PUFFIN BOOKS

Finn's Island

Eileen Dunlop was born in Alloa, Scotland, and educated in Alloa and Edinburgh. She lives in Scotland with her husband, Antony Kamm. Scotland is the theme and setting for each of the several books she has written.

Best wishes. Ian

Eileen Dunlop

Oct '94

Finn's Island

Eileen Dunlop

PUFFIN BOOKS

For Mabel George

PUFFIN BOOKS

Published by the Penguin Group
Penguin Books Ltd, 27 Wrights Lane, London W8 5TZ, England
Penguin Books USA Inc., 375 Hudson Street, New York, New York 10014, USA
Penguin Books Australia Ltd, Ringwood, Victoria, Australia
Penguin Books Canada Ltd, 10 Alcorn Avenue, Toronto, Ontario, Canada M4V 3B2
Penguin Books (NZ) Ltd, 182–190 Wairau Road, Auckland 10, New Zealand

Penguin Books Ltd, Registered Offices: Harmondsworth, Middlesex, England

First published by Blackie and Son Ltd 1991
Published in Puffin Books 1994
1 3 5 7 9 10 8 6 4 2

Printed in England by Clays Ltd, St Ives plc

Contents

Hirsay

Tigh na Finn
Cnoc Ruadh
Hirsay Bay
Hirsay village
Hamasgeir
Pool of Seals
SHEEP SOUND
Pirates
Fulmar Beacon
Blue Men Tribe
Eilean nan Gall

Leaving Hirsay

The Island had never looked more beautiful than it did on that last morning, and that was part of the pain. It might have been easier, Jamie thought, to leave on a bitter grey day, when the weather at least would have kept faith with the darkness in his heart. Instead, as he scrambled barefoot up the heathery slope of Cnoc Ruadh, the Red Hill, sun and cloud patched the land with light and shade, while white sea birds swooped sparkling over the foam-flecked, navy-blue sea. Jamie listened to their hoarse, torn crying, as if it were music that he would never hear again.

It was a long way up. The Red Hill rose more than a thousand feet above the sea, and when at last Jamie reached the platform of rough vegetation which was its summit, he was sweating and out of breath. Flopping down on the grass, he closed his eyes, and filled his lungs with the Island's air, salt from the sea, scented from the heather, sharp from the acid droppings of countless fulmars, gulls and gannets. These birds lived on the cliffs which sliced through the Red Hill, sudden and terrifyingly high, only a short distance from where Jamie lay.

He stayed quite still for a while, feeling himself cooled and dried by the wind that blew constantly over the Island, opposing the warmth of the September sun.

Then, when he had recovered his breath, he sat up and looked around him. For this was what he had come here to do, to fix in his memory for ever the Island where he had lived all the twelve years of his life, and which he was to leave that evening, for ever. Down in the village, where the twenty-eight Islanders were packing the last of their poor belongings, there was brave talk of how they would come back next year, to spend the summer months in the homes they were abandoning. Perhaps, for some of them, it made the despair of leaving more tolerable, but not for Jamie Lochlan. He knew that he would never come back. He had been dreading this day for months, and he could not bear to think of living through it a second time.

Looking down, Jamie could see the tiny village of grey, turf-hatted cottages, clinging to the stony rim of Hirsay Bay. On the causeway between the village and the jetty, minute figures toiled along, weighed down by boxes and bundles that had to be taken to the boat. Behind the cottages, across a walled garden that belonged to everyone, stood the little white church and school, and then the bleak graveyard. Beyond that were the fields which, in former years, would by now have been yellow with the stubble of harvest safely in. But this year, knowing in their hearts that they could not live on Hirsay through another winter, the Islanders had planted no crops in the spring. Already weeds were beginning to green the dark earth. Everything else was hillside, stained purple now with heather, and the sea. You could not go anywhere on Hirsay without the sound of the sea in your ears, howling and crashing in winter, talkative in summer, carrying on its back the screaming birds, and the wind with its many voices.

Jamie looked out to sea. Away to the west it stretched,

mile after mile, the nearest landfall America. A man from Hirsay had gone to America once, but had never returned to tell his tale. Jamie's voyage would be eastward, no great distance, but to a place as remote to him as America was to Christopher Columbus. It was hidden behind a long, soft blue line which, on a clear day like this, you could see crayonned on the horizon – islands, called the Outer Hebrides. Behind the blue line was a country called Scotland, and in that country a city called Glasgow, where Jamie was going to live. He was not sure what a city was, but he would find out tomorrow.

The sun was turning into the west now, and Jamie knew that he would soon have to go down.

'Keep your eye on the sun,' his mother had warned him when he left her. 'The ship will sail at seven, and I don't want to leave you behind.'

He supposed that she was teasing, for certainly she would not leave him behind, her only son, and she a widow since his father was drowned last winter at the fishing. So he had laughed, and promised to be back in good time. Her jokes had been more amusing before the bad days came.

He could see the ship now, an angular, dark shape lying at anchor out in the Bay. She was HMS *Bonaventure*, sent by His Majesty's Government to evacuate the people of Hirsay, who could no longer endure life on an Island too small and unimportant even to be marked on the map. The young men had been leaving to work on the mainland for years. Now sickness and poor harvests had done for those who remained. They would not come back, let them say what they liked now.

Jamie got up, and let the wind blow him across the summit, until he was within a few feet of the cliff edge, on the north side of the Island. Then he got down on his hands and knees, and crawled cautiously forward, dropping right down on his stomach before he dared to look over the rim. His throat tightened, and instinctively his fingers clutched at the clumps of coarse grass which grew along the margin of the rock.

The drop was horrifying, down a jagged precipice to the violent green sea, which growled and sucked hungrily around broken fangs of granite far below. Thousands of sea birds filled the air, like feathers shaken out of a pillow, floating with the daredevil arrogance of creatures made safe by wings. Jamie had wanted to look, but he could not look for long. Carefully he squirmed back, and when he thought it was safe, got shakily to his feet.

It was time to leave now, because his mother was easily made anxious. But before he went, Jamie looked around on top of the Red Hill for some treasures to take with him. He found a white feather, a smooth black stone, a strand of grey sheep's wool, and a brown snail shell with a cream whorl. Then, stooping down, he pulled a handful of pathan, the magical little star-flower of Hirsay. Grey-leaved and white-bloomed, it grew only in this high, windswept place. It cured disease, and it would keep you safe, wherever you had to go.

1 An Island in his Mind

'We should have gone to live on the Island,' Finn said.

It was a remark more than likely to irritate his father, and it did. Mr Lochlan was not the kind of man who shouted and banged about, but the crease between his black eyebrows deepened, and there was exasperation in his voice as he replied, 'It's more than sixty years since people lived on the Island. They left because they were starving. We're not starving – yet. Whatever our problems are here, they're nothing compared with what they would have been if we'd been daft enough to try to live on Hirsay. Don't be such a fool, Finn.'

He rose abruptly, and stalked out of the kitchen on his long, thin legs, leaving Finn sitting at the table, with his homework spread out in front of him.

'Oh dear,' said Finn. 'I've said the wrong thing.'

His grandmother, who was sitting by the fire with her knitting, turned her untidy grey head and looked at him, half incredulous and half amused. She was tired, creaking with rheumatism, grieving still over the death of her husband, and worried sick about her son. But Finn made her laugh. He was so tactless, and always so surprised when his tactlessness made anyone cross.

'Well, yes,' she agreed, turning her needles round, and beginning to knit in the other direction. 'When you've just announced that the roof's leaking, and the hens won't lay, and you have corns and an overdraft at the Bank, the last thing you want to hear is that it's all your own fault for not going to live somewhere else. Especially when you know you couldn't have gone to live there anyway.'

'Grandpa said we could have gone to Hirsay, Granny,' Finn said.

But Mrs Lochlan was not going to be drawn into an argument about this. Sometimes she wished she had never heard the word, 'Hirsay'.

'He was wrong,' she said quietly. 'Now finish your homework and go and say goodnight to your Dad. It's time you were up to bed.'

'All right. What's eight nines, plus fifteen, minus four?'

'Eighty-three,' she replied automatically. She had been a teacher, long ago.

Finn wrote the number down.

'There, then. That's me finished,' he said, flipping his book shut, and beginning to pack his school bag, ready for the morning. 'Do I have to go and say goodnight to Dad, Granny?'

'You know the answer to that question,' was the reply.

Mr Lochlan was in his study, across the draughty passage from the kitchen. It was a small but cosy room, with lots of bookshelves, a desk with a lamp, some pictures of Greek temples, and a comfortable armchair. It was very different from the kitchen, which had a bare stone floor, threadbare curtains, and furniture which had been second-hand when Finn's grandparents married in 1943.

It was perhaps unusual for a poor farmer to have

such a study, but Mr Lochlan had not always been a poor farmer. Until two years ago, he had been a teacher of Latin and Greek at a school in Glasgow. When they closed down his department because all the pupils chose Computer Studies instead of Latin, he had been made redundant. It was called 'early retirement' – far too early for him, since he was only forty. He was given a small pension, and a sum of money to compensate him for the loss of his job. Using this, and the proceeds from the sale of his Glasgow house, he had bought Corumbeg, a tiny hill farm in Glenaire, thirty miles from Perth.

Mr Lochlan said that the move was for Finn's sake. It was better for a boy to grow up in the country, eating wholesome food and drinking uncontaminated water. Besides, Finn wanted to be a country boy. But it also had something to do with a man called Virgil, whom Mr Lochlan greatly admired. Virgil had written poems in Latin, including one about the Wooden Horse of Troy, and he had owned a farm in Italy. Finn knew this because Granny sometimes remarked that she supposed it was warmer on Virgil's farm, or that she hoped Virgil had better success with his cauliflowers. Virgil had certainly had more success with his poems than Mr Lochlan, who wrote lots, but had not, so far, found anyone who was keen to publish them.

He was writing a poem now – it kept his mind off his worries about the farm – but he put down his pen when Finn came in, and looked at him with his dark, reticent eyes.

'Come to say goodnight?' he asked.

'Yes.'

'Sorry I was snappy.'

'Sorry I was a fool.'

Every night they apologised to each other for something. It had become habitual, but it didn't bring them any closer together.

'Done your homework?'

'Yes.'

'Goodnight then, son.'

'Goodnight, Dad.'

That was all. The same every night. Finn left the study, groped for the switch to turn on the light on the landing, and went upstairs. Thankfully he opened the door of his bedroom, and stepped into another world.

Until two years ago, when his father had lost his job, Finn had lived all his life in the city. A child of the busy streets and public parks, he had walked to school alongside thundering traffic, and played in a grassless schoolyard. When his father, genuinely hoping to delight him, had announced that they were moving to the country, he had been angered by Finn's lack of enthusiasm.

'You can do nothing that pleases that boy,' Mr Lochlan had remarked bitterly to his parents, who had lived with him ever since Finn's mother had died of leukaemia when Finn was barely two.

But the truth was that Corumbeg was as far as Glasgow was from the place where Finn really wanted to be – the Island of Hirsay, furthest of the far Hebrides, from which his grandfather, and twenty-eight other Islanders, had been evacuated on 5th September, 1929. No one had lived on Hirsay since, apart from the English businessman who owned it and spent a few weeks there every summer, and the naturalists whom he allowed to study the wildlife of the Island. But old Jamie Lochlan had never forgotten his childhood there, and it was he who had filled Finn's imagination with tales of Hirsay, making it sound the most marvellous place where a boy could live. Finn's father was wrong in thinking that Finn wanted to be a country boy. Finn wanted to be an Islander, a boy of Hirsay, like his grandfather more than sixty years before.

When Finn closed his bedroom door behind him, it was into the world of the Island that he stepped. Other children had posters of pop stars and pictures of football teams on their bedroom walls, but Finn was indifferent to these things. On the one wall of his room which did not slope steeply under the roof, he had pinned up the large map of Hirsay which he and his grandfather had made and coloured together, showing the bays and headlands, hills, cliffs, rocks and skerries of that distant isle. Finn had collected pictures of the sea birds that lived on the cliffs, and had made beautiful drawings of fish, flowers, animals and insects. He had mounted these on black card, and stuck them up around the map.

Since the death of his grandfather six months ago, Finn had begun to add to the map features which were not actually there, although he suspected that Grandpa would not have approved of this. There was now a fort on the Red Hill, which he named Tigh na Finn, Finn's House. There was also an offshore island called Eilean nan Gall, Isle of the Strangers, and a lighthouse which he had to call Fulmar Beacon, because really he knew scarcely any Gaelic at all.

Tonight, when he had taken off his clothes and put on his pyjamas, he fetched a pencil, and drew on the map a little galleon, riding at anchor in Sheep Sound, on the other side of the Island from Hirsay Bay. He wrote the word, 'Pirates', beside it, then climbed into bed, because he could hear Granny's feet on the uncarpeted stair. She opened the door and came in, thin and shivery in her old brown jersey and tweed skirt. Although it was only late August, the northern nights were growing chilly, and she hated the cold. As usual, she was carrying a tray with two mugs of cocoa. Sometimes she stayed, and they drank the cocoa together, but tonight she handed him his mug and said, 'I'm away to my bed, dearie. I'm tired out. Remember to get up and clean your teeth.'

Finn knew that what she meant was, 'I've had a bad day missing Grandpa. I'd rather be by myself when I feel like this.' He felt sorry for her, but he did not know how to comfort her. She had never visited Hirsay, and the Island meant nothing to her.

'Yes, all right. Goodnight, Granny,' he said.

'Goodnight, my dear.'

Finn gulped his cocoa, and felt guilty because he was glad she hadn't stayed. But he was in a hurry to put out the light. For that was when he could curl up in a ball, with his hot-water bottle between his thighs, close his eyes tight, and begin to live in what he called the 'Hirsay Story'.

He was still Finn Lochlan, but he had gone back in time to the nineteen twenties, and he was his grandfather's younger brother, and closest friend. They looked very alike, blue-eyed and fair, as you would expect boys to be who were descended from a Viking, a son of the king of Norway, Mac Righ Lochlainn. They lived with their mother in a stone-walled cottage in a tiny village, close to the shore of Hirsay Bay. Finn and Jamie – for you could hardly call your big brother Grandpa – enjoyed a wonderful life together. They went fishing in their own boat, the *Kittiwake*, and climbed the cliffs to collect sea birds' eggs for their

16

supper. They helped with the sheep shearing and the barley harvest, and went shrimping on the rocks in the evening sunshine.

Recently, they had been leading the other Islanders in strengthening the fort on the Red Hill, for fear of attack by the Blue Men, sinister folk who had recently appeared on Eilean nan Gall. And this morning, Jamie had come running home, to report that a pirate ship, the *Black Snake*, had dropped anchor in Sheep Sound.

'Bring your dagger, and Dad's old rifle, Finn,' he had ordered. 'We may have a fight on our hands.'

Usually, Finn fell asleep at the most exciting bit, but that didn't matter. The next night he could carry on if he wanted to, from where he had left off. Or he could change the story, or even start a new one. And he could forget the unhappy grown-ups with whom he lived, his guilt because he did not share their worries and disappointments, and his own misery because he would never see Grandpa again.

2 News

When Finn came out of school next day into the mellow, late summer sunshine, he could see his father sitting in his ramshackle old Land-rover on the other side of the road. Even when you couldn't see his constantly tapping hands and feet, Mr Lochlan looked fidgety. Finn knew that his dark moustache had been twitching, and his tongue clicking impatiently, ever since he had switched off the engine five minutes before. Finn was never late out of school – he knew better – yet he always felt he was wasting his father's time, that his father had better things to do than to drive down four miles from Corumbeg to fetch him.

This seemed unfair to Finn. He did not, after all, go to Yett School five days a week because he wanted to. It was quite a pleasant place, and Finn could do the work well enough to avoid trouble. But nothing that happened there really interested him. He wished that he had been a boy on Hirsay, where as often as not there was no school at all, because the namby-pamby teachers from the mainland couldn't stand the Island's hard, isolated life. After a few months they packed their bags and left, and then the school had to be closed until the next innocent arrived. Grandpa had arrived in Glasgow at the age of twelve barely able to read and write – which might have been a disadvantage in

Glasgow, Finn thought, but wouldn't have mattered on Hirsay. On Hirsay, there were more important things to do.

As he had expected, by the time he had got across the road, and hoisted himself into the back of the dirty Land-rover, Mr Lochlan was tutting audibly.

'Where have you been?' he demanded crossly, as he revved the engine, and swung out sharply onto the narrow country road. 'It's nearly twenty to four.'

Finn resisted the temptation to reply that he had spent the day working down a coal-mine, and had got stuck in the cage coming to the surface. There would be something else to apologise for before bedtime.

'I came out as soon as Mrs Ritchie rang the bell,' he said. 'May I have a toffee, Dad?'

Mr Lochlan reached into a box on the shelf in front of him, and tossed a couple of toffees over his shoulder. In some ways, he was quite generous.

He drove, and Finn chewed, in silence, until they had left the little grey school and the village far behind. Beyond the spruce plantation, Mr Lochlan turned right, and began the long, bumpy ascent, first through grassy fields, then over moorland royally purple with flowering heather, towards Corumbeg. From far away, Finn could see the white farmhouse with its hooded upstairs windows, riding above the heathery waves. Smoke curled up lazily from the low kitchen chimney, and it looked attractive until you got close enough to see the peeling walls, and dilapidated farm buildings. Finn got out to open the boundary gate, and when he got back in, Mr Lochlan said, 'I had a letter this morning.'

'Oh dear,' said Finn, trying to sound sympathetic. 'Was it from the Income Tax people again?'

19

'No. We're going to have a visitor.'

'A visitor,' echoed Finn. There had been no visitors at Corumbeg since Grandpa's funeral, and precious few before that. Then an awful thought occurred. 'It's not Auntie Phyllis, is it?'

Auntie Phyllis was Mr Lochlan's elder sister, and probably the bossiest woman in the world. Mr Lochlan uttered the snort that was the nearest he ever got to a laugh.

'Lord, no. It's not as bad as that,' he replied. 'It's a student – a chap from the Agricultural College in town. He has to spend two months working on a small farm as part of his training. A man I know who lectures at the College wrote some time ago to ask if I would take him. It seemed quite a good idea. He gets experience, and I get some money for his board and lodging. And,' he added hopefully, 'maybe he'll be able to give me some advice.'

It was at moments like this that Finn was torn between exasperation and pity for his father. If he was so helpless that he really needed a young student to tell him what to do, perhaps it was just as well that he hadn't gone to live on Hirsay. There he'd have needed twenty times the resourcefulness required to live at Corumbeg. Maybe he should have stayed in Glasgow, and spent his redundancy money on a grocer's shop.

'Where's the student going to sleep?' Finn asked.

'In the room next to yours. Granny will air the bed, and I'll put in the hall table for him to write on.'

'When's he coming?'

'On Sunday evening.'

'What's his name?'

Mr Lochlan took longer to answer this question. 'It was in the letter,' he said at last. 'Wait a minute.

20

Cooper. Yes, that's it. Douglas Cooper.'

Of course, Finn realised, his father was not in the least interested in the student's name. If the Hunchback of Notre-Dame turned up on Sunday, Mr Lochlan wouldn't bat an eyelid, as long as he knew how to get the hens to lay, and stop rabbits from guzzling the vegetables. And as long as there was money to be made from having him at Corumbeg.

3   A Patch of Damp

Finn did not spend a lot of time thinking about Douglas Cooper, because his mind was busy with developments in the Hirsay Story. The pirates were planning to take over the Island, and make it a safe haven for themselves and other buccaneers, so Jamie and Finn had to decide what action to take. There was a bit of an argument about this, over dinner in the little cottage. Finn thought they should row out to the *Black Snake* under cover of night, board her and set fire to her. Jamie rather favoured setting traps among the rocks, and ambushing the pirates when they came ashore.

These exciting matters diverted Finn's attention, as they were meant to do, from what was going on around him. From time to time, however, when Mr Lochlan and Granny were at their gloomiest, it did cross Finn's mind that it might be fun to have a young person about the farm, someone who would whistle as he went about his work, and tell a joke occasionally.

On Saturday morning, Mr Lochlan went off early to Perth, to buy the next week's food supply at the supermarket. Hopes of self-sufficiency at Corumbeg had faded, and while the hens were on strike, even eggs had to be brought from the town. It was fortunate that Granny had her old age pension and some savings. Mr Lochlan said he would pay her back when things improved, a promise which, Finn noticed, she wisely ignored.

Finn had intended to spend the day in his room, painting a picture of the Blue Men of Eilean nan Gall, who had become powerful wizards, luring sailors onto the rocks with the irresistible music of their harps. At breakfast-time, however, Granny told him that painting would have to wait until the afternoon, since she needed him to help her get the spare room ready for Douglas Cooper's arrival on Sunday.

'It will need a thorough clean,' she said, 'if we're not to be disgraced. The cobwebs are like lace curtains, and the dust is like a fall of snow. I'll need you to go up the ladder and wash the woodwork, while I hoover the floor and make the bed. All right?'

'Sure,' agreed Finn. He was fond of Granny, who made the best tomato soup and sausage hot-pot imaginable. And even if she did complain about everything, and have huffy silences that rivalled his father's, you could have a laugh with her once in a while. Finn could never remember having a laugh with his father. So now he said, 'Don't carry up anything heavy. I'll get the ladder out of the woodshed.'

No amount of hard work could have made the spare room beautiful, but after three hours of scrubbing and dusting it was transformed from a dirty, neglected place to a clean, if still shabby one. Finn hung fresh striped curtains at the window, and Granny, panting mightily, put laundered sheets and blankets on the bed. There was a crack in one of the tiny window-panes, and an ugly damp patch on the faded wallpaper behind the bed, but when a red rag rug from Granny's room had been unrolled on the bare wooden floor, the effect was quite cheerful. Finn found a fringed mat to hide the scratches on the chest of drawers, and a pair of book-ends with owls carved on them, which he put on the table his father had carried up yesterday from the hall.

'How's that, then?' he asked, standing back to admire what they had done.

Granny, who had sat down on the bed to rest her legs, pursed her lips critically, then nodded her tousled grey head.

'We can't do more,' was her judgement. 'Pity about the mark on the wall, but that can't be helped. This house has damp in its bones, like me.'

Finn frowned at the grey blotch. It looked like an island, which was probably what gave him the idea. 'I know,' he said. 'We could cover it with a picture. Hang on, Granny.'

He went quickly to his own room next door, pulled out an old suitcase from under his bed, and found a page which he had cut from last year's *Scotland's Heritage* calendar. It was a large coloured photograph of Hirsay Bay, showing the sea, and the ruined village, and the Red Hill sweeping up majestically into a cap of mist. Finn took four thumb-tacks from a tin in his desk drawer, and hurried back to the spare room.

'See?' he said triumphantly, as he scrambled over the bed, unrolled the picture, and stabbed the tacks through its corners. 'Just the right size to cover the damp patch. Looks great, doesn't it?'

Old Mrs Lochlan glanced wearily at the Island of other people's dreams, then she turned and looked into Finn's face. But she did not answer his question. Easing herself carefully off the bed, she straightened the quilt, picked up her dusters, and opened the door.

'Let's have our lunch,' she said. 'How do you fancy a bowl of tomato soup and a bacon sandwich?'

4   One Man and his Dog

At six o'clock on Sunday evening, when the sun was perching like a silver hoop on the rim of Corum Hill, Finn sat on the yard gate, watching the car as it approached slowly up the winding field track. Emerging from the trees at the bottom of the valley it was just a car, then it became a blue car, its windscreen bright as it caught the reflection of the sun. By the time it got to the boundary gate, it was recognisable as a Ford Escort, but the figure who got out to open and shut the gate was still too far away to have any distinguishing features. Only when the car finally bounced through the yard gate did Finn see a bearded face, and a large hand waving to him through the side window. Quickly he shut the gate, and ran to stand beside his father and Granny on the kitchen doorstep. The car rocked to a halt over the bumpy cobblestones, and out of it climbed the largest man Finn had ever seen.

It wasn't just his size that was surprising either, although he was as tall as Mr Lochlan, and twice as broad. They had all assumed that a student would be a young man, perhaps twenty, or twenty-one. Douglas Cooper was twice as old as that, a giant with a tanned, weather-worn face, and thick black hair already laced with threads of grey. The muscles of his legs pressed against the brown corduroy of his trousers, and his green shirt was like a small tent.

Mr Lochlan advanced to shake hands with him, casting a thin shadow on the yard floor.

'Like a giraffe and an elephant,' whispered Finn to Granny, who said, 'Sh!' automatically, but couldn't help laughing at the aptness of the joke.

Then the newcomer was shaking hands with Granny '— Just Douglas, not Mr Cooper, if you don't mind —' and grinning down at Finn from a great height. 'Hi, Finn. Thanks for opening the gate. Nice place, this.'

But Finn was looking past him, his eyes drawn by a movement in the back of the car.

'There's a dog,' he said, in surprise.

'Yes. It's Shep,' said Douglas, going to open the car door, and let the animal jump down. 'I'm trying to train him for the sheep, and I thought maybe he could learn a bit working with your dog. You don't mind, do you?' He looked rather uncertainly at Mr Lochlan's unsmiling face, while the collie ran straight to Finn, and rubbed itself against his knees.

'Not at all,' said Mr Lochlan, with stiff politeness. This hardly seemed the time to start explaining to Douglas Cooper why he didn't keep a dog, or to ask who was to provide food for such a large, healthy young animal.

Finn, however, was delighted. He bent down to fondle Shep's soft ears, and wished he had a piece of chocolate to give him.

Supper that night was the most pleasant meal Finn could remember at Corumbeg since Grandpa died. Normally, meals were eaten in silence, the coming together of three related people only emphasising their isolation from one another. But tonight, it was different. Mr Lochlan, mollified by the appearance in the kitchen of a large box containing tins of dog food, had decided to be civil. Granny was pleased by Douglas's appreciation of her chicken casserole, while Finn was full of enthusiasm for this warm, friendly man, and for the dog lying on the hearth-rug, watching them with alert brown eyes.

They learned that Douglas was married to Bess, and had one son, Chris, who was eleven. Douglas had been a teacher too, but had decided to give up teaching when Bess got a job in medical research at the University.

'Bess is the brains in our family,' he said without envy, 'and she earns a lot of money. So she's paying the mortgage until I get through College, then we're going to try to get a place in the country too. We've buzzed around far too much, and it's time to settle down. I couldn't have started straight from teaching as you did, Colin,' he added innocently to Mr Lochlan. 'I've always wanted to farm, but I didn't know the first thing about it. You were brought up to it, I suppose?'

'My father was a gardener,' said Mr Lochlan shortly, and soon afterwards remembered that he had some paperwork to do in the study.

'Fancy a walk before it gets dark?' Douglas asked Finn, when Granny had refused his help with the washing-up.

'Not on your first night,' she said firmly, 'although at other times I shan't say no.'

And Finn, who never took walks, said he'd love to, and rushed away to put on a jersey, and change his shoes.

A soft silvery line, defining the purple mass of Corum Hill, was all that was left of the sunset, but day and night were still in the balance as Finn and Douglas closed the kitchen door behind them. With Shep stepping neatly at their heels, they made their way up through the turnip field, over the stile, and onto the hillside. It was the dying hour of a beautiful late summer day, chilly, blue and clear as glass. Douglas turned to gaze out over the darkening swell of the Ochils, then down into the valley, where the lights of Yett were pushing up through the dusk, like a parcel of golden stars. He took a deep gulp of air, breathed out slowly, and said, 'Fantastic.' Then he bent down to attach a leather lead to Shep's collar. 'He doesn't have much experience yet,' he explained, 'and I don't want to start my time here with my dog in trouble for chasing sheep. How many lambs did your Dad get this year, Finn?'

'I haven't a clue,' Finn replied.

If Douglas was surprised by this response, he didn't say so, and they walked along between a dry stone wall and the Bindle Burn, a busy little stream which raced gabbling over stones and around dark cushions of grass. Beyond, the ghostly movement of sheep on the moorland broke the stillness of the northern dusk.

Presently, Douglas tried again.

'How many sheep does your Dad have, Finn?' he enquired.

Finn had found a long stick, and was running it along the lichened surface of the wall.

'I'm not sure,' he said. 'Maybe about a hundred? He doesn't do the sheep himself.'

'Doesn't do the sheep himself?' repeated Douglas, and Finn could sense his puzzlement. 'What does that mean, exactly?'

Finn tried to explain.

'Well, Mr Curtis at Middle Corum has a big flock, and

Dad pays him – something – for Tam Orr to look after ours as well. Tam Orr is Mr Curtis's shepherd.'

There was silence after this, and Finn knew that Douglas was finding the explanation hard to understand. He would find it even harder to understand, Finn thought, if he had known that Mr Lochlan was actually borrowing money from his old mother to buy food from a Perth supermarket, while giving a large slice of his precious pension to Mr Curtis every month, for Tam Orr to do a job he could easily have done himself. If he'd had the gumption, and a good dog.

Still, when Douglas said carefully, 'So – what does he actually do?,' loyalty prevented Finn from saying, 'Pretends he's Virgil.'

Instead he said, 'Oh, the vegetables, you know, and the hens. And he's got four pigs to fatten for the market. He's kept very busy.'

Douglas said, 'I see,' but Finn knew he didn't see at all.

'Anyway,' he went on brightly, 'Tam can tell you all you want to know about sheep. I heard Dad telling Granny that he's arranged with Mr Curtis for you to have some lessons. And he's hoping you'll be able to tell him what you've learned at College about pigs and hens.'

He heard Douglas laughing softly in the half-dark. They had come to a gate in the end of the wall, and Finn opened it to let them through. While he was chaining it up again, Douglas let Shep off the lead. Then he said casually, 'And what about you, Finn? Will you be working with us on the farm?'

'No way,' said Finn bluntly. 'I'm not interested in that sort of thing.' And because, much as he liked

Douglas, he did not yet know him well enough to mention Hirsay, he was obliged to answer the next question, 'What are you interested in?' by muttering vaguely, 'Oh, drawing, I suppose. And birds.'

'Well, you'll see plenty of birds in these parts,' observed Douglas pleasantly, as they walked down through the shadowy fields towards the house. 'What's the most exciting you've ever seen?'

Finn had seen a kestrel, a barn owl, a Siberian thrush, and a kingfisher down by the river Aire. But he said, 'A seagull.' Because for him, it was true. No bird of this countryside had the power to rouse in him the longing he felt when he saw those white, ice-eyed birds, flying inland, it was said, to escape storms at sea. Gulls constantly skimmed the ocean around Hirsay, and their raucous cries sounded to Finn like familiar music to an exile in a foreign land.

5   A Traveller's Tale

Much to his disappointment, Finn did not see a great deal of Douglas during the next few days. When he got up and came downstairs at half-past seven, Douglas had already eaten his breakfast and gone out. Mr Lochlan had arranged with Mr Curtis that Douglas would spend the first week of his stay with Tam Orr, learning about the sheep, and Tam was an early riser. Shep was also out, learning his job with Tam's two sheepdogs, Tosh and Tray.

Douglas usually came in at half-past five, and spent an hour in the study discussing the day's work with Mr Lochlan. Not long after that, it was time for supper. Then Finn had homework to do, and so, he discovered, had Douglas. As soon as he had helped Granny with the washing-up, he disappeared to his own room to do some studying. This was his final year, and he had a lot of revision to do.

So it was only at the supper table that there was time for conversation, and conversation was not quite the right word for it. Because in a way, all three Lochlans lived on islands, cut off from everyone else, it was left to Douglas to do most of the talking – not that he seemed to mind this. He had many tales to tell, which left the Lochlans breathless with astonishment. His size and age were only the beginning of the surprises this stranger had to offer them.

Although he described himself as a teacher, Douglas's career had been as different from Mr Lochlan's as it was possible to imagine. He had spent most of the last twenty years teaching in remote corners of the world, Nepal, the Highlands of Kenya, Peru. This had provided him with enough money to pay for his real passion, climbing mountains. The Lochlans learned that he had climbed in the Himalayas, and the Andes, and Mount Elgon in Kenya. He told them about treks through the Siwaliks, foothills of the Himalayas. He described strange, rare animals he had seen, Hanuman langur monkeys in Nepal, chinchillas and a puma in Peru. He told of narrow escapes on windswept glaciers, and the feeling of joy when you finally got to the top.

'And how did your wife like such an adventurous life?' asked Granny one evening. She would not have liked it at all. Although she enjoyed Douglas's stories, she thought it sounded worse than living on Hirsay, which was saying something.

'Oh, it suited Bess perfectly,' said Douglas happily. 'She had a job at that time working for the Science Museum, tracking down rare plants and photographing them. She wrote a book about her work, and made a television series – about three years ago, it must have been. You didn't happen to see it?'

The Lochlans had to confess that there was no television at Corumbeg. Nobody missed it. There had been no television on Hirsay, or on Virgil's farm.

'So – why did you come back?' Finn wanted to know. Although he had no more desire to live in Nepal than he had to live at Corumbeg, he reckoned that living in Glasgow, and going to Agricultural College, must be tame compared with living in such outlandish places.

'Because of Chris, really,' Douglas explained. 'He was born at Katmandu, in Nepal, and he's lived with us in all the places where we've worked, but a couple of years ago we realised that he needed a settled spell of education, so it was time to pack our bags and come home. Anyway, Bess and I are getting older, and we want a quieter life.' He paused, then added, 'Chris, of course, is finding new challenges of his own.'

Finn helped himself to a second helping of apple sponge, and wished he'd kept his mouth shut. He had noticed early on that however Douglas's stories started, they always got round to Chris in the end. Chris had climbed Schiehallion and Ben Nevis, and cycled from Glasgow to Inverness. He had been rock-climbing in Wales, and had taken part in a yacht race across the Irish Sea. Last Christmas he had camped on Rannoch Moor in the snow with his mum and dad, and he was learning to ski. Finn thought that Douglas was wonderful, and that his traveller's tales had turned the old, boring supper times into magic hours. But he wished he would shut up about Chris. Every time Chris was mentioned, Finn tried to divert Douglas by asking bright questions about the climbs in the wind-shrieking mountains, but Douglas always got round to Chris again in the end. Chris's exploits obviously meant much more to him than his own.

If anyone had said to Finn, 'You're jealous,' he would have denied it angrily, pointing out that he had no desire to do any of the things which Chris Cooper apparently did so well. Which was true. But, because he had never had to share Grandpa, he had never had the experience of hearing a person he cared about speaking with warm preference of someone else. This was what was happening now, and it hurt.

Each night, when he went upstairs to bed, and saw a strip of light shining under Douglas's door, Finn was tempted to knock, and go in for a chat. But Granny had warned him not to do this, and besides, he wasn't yet sure enough of Douglas to risk it. Finn knew how upset he would be if he were snubbed. Late on Thursday night, however, when he got up to go to the loo before turning out his light, Finn saw that Douglas's door was open. So he stopped, leaned on the doorpost in his pyjamas, and said, 'Hi.'

'Hi to you,' responded Douglas pleasantly, so Finn ventured in.

The spare room looked warm and comfortable, with Douglas's belongings strewn around. He had brought his own radio and reading-lamp, and had used the owl book-ends to support a row of books on top of the chest of drawers. He had risen from his table, which was awash with notebooks and sheets of file paper, and was standing in his shirt sleeves in the middle of the floor. He grimaced at Finn, stretched his arms above his head, and said, 'I'm not having a good night. Can't seem to concentrate.' Then, to Finn's delight, he pointed to the picture which was pinned over the damp patch on the wall. 'My eyes keep wandering to this photograph of Hirsay Bay,' he told him. 'Impressive, isn't it?'

Finn wouldn't have mentioned the subject without this encouragement, but now he just had to tell.

'My Grandpa lived there when he was a boy,' he said proudly. 'He was evacuated with the last Islanders in 1929, when he was twelve.'

Douglas made the right response. Widening his brown eyes in astonishment, he made a whistling sound, then said, 'Was he really? That's very distinguished. And I'm speaking to his grandson!' Finn basked in the glory of Grandpa's kinship.

'He was descended from a Viking,' he said.

But Douglas had turned back to the picture, and now he surprised Finn by saying, 'Of course, this photograph must have been taken some time ago. It isn't quite like this now.'

'Isn't it?' asked Finn uncertainly.

'No. Here —' Douglas leaned over the bed, and indicated a smudge on the hillside just above the ruined cottages '— Mr Ackerley has rebuilt the Manse as a house for himself, and here, just behind it, he's had the school rebuilt as a hostel for people who want to stay on the Island for a while. Ex-army beds and a chemical toilet, but it's OK.'

There was a strong clue here, but Finn failed to pick it up. 'Who's Mr Ackerley?' he enquired.

'The man from London who owns the Island. Very posh, and very rich, but a nice chap, all the same.'

Still Finn didn't understand. The truth was staring him in the face, but perhaps it was too stupendous to be taken in.

'You've read a lot about it,' he said, making it sound both a question and a statement.

Then it was spelled out for him.

'Yes, I have. And I've been there, twice. Bess and I helped to rebuild the school.'

Never, in all his life, had Finn been less pleased to see Granny and her blessed mugs of cocoa. Just at this dramatic moment, she popped up in the doorway, bringing one to Douglas. She was not pleased to see Finn, either. He was shoo-ed off to the bathroom, and warned that he had better not have to be called twice

36

in the morning.

But as he fled along the landing, he heard Douglas calling after him, 'Tomorrow, Finn. I'll tell you about it tomorrow!'

6   Going to Perth

Finn was frequently in trouble for day-dreaming in school, but the next day was worse than usual. How could he concentrate on unimportant things like Maths and reading, and making a model of Yett Tower, when a man who had been twice on Hirsay was herding sheep on Corum Hill? It seemed like a miracle that of all the students who might have come to Corumbeg, Mr Lochlan had been given the one who was a living link between Finn and the Island of his desire. It was all he could think about, and he longed for the day to end, so that he could get home, rush up to the hill to find Douglas, and hear the account which Granny had so provokingly spoiled the night before. Even more often than usual, Mrs Ritchie had to say, 'Wake up, Finn!' or, 'Come on, Finn. You're dreaming again!'

When the bell finally released him at half-past three however, a pleasant surprise awaited Finn. Douglas, not his father, had come to fetch him. Eagerly he raced over to where the big man stood beside his blue Ford, chatting to two of the village mothers who had come to meet their children. Mr Lochlan never got out of the car, and he never spoke to anyone.

It had been a bright, breezy day. Douglas was wearing a green padded jerkin over a checked shirt, with the sleeves rolled up to his elbows, revealing massive, hairy forearms. He greeted Finn cheerfully.

'Hi, there. Hop in the back.'

Finn scrambled into the car on the passenger side. On the other side, the driver's seat was pushed all the way back, to make room for Douglas's long legs. When he had eased himself in, he seemed to occupy the space in all directions.

'Too wee for me, this car,' he remarked, as he started the engine. 'Next time I'm going to treat myself to a bus.'

'You're facing the wrong way,' Finn informed him.

'No, I'm not,' Douglas replied. 'I'm on my way to Perth to get supplies. I told Colin I'd pick you up and take you with me. OK?'

'You bet,' said Finn. 'What sort of supplies?'

Douglas recited his shopping list as they drove out of Yett Wood into the sunshine, and headed up the Glen Road towards the motorway.

'Whitewash. Wire netting and wire for fencing. Nails. Colin has decided that the steading needs attention, and that's to be our next job.'

Finn uttered a snort, and would have been offended if anyone had told him he sounded exactly like his father. But Mr Lochlan had been living for two years with derelict barns and sagging fences, and Finn doubted that he was the one who suddenly thought they needed attention. However, if Douglas could make suggestions in a way that made Mr Lochlan think he was having bright ideas for himself, that was all to the good. Mr Lochlan seemed to be a little brighter generally; he snorted more, and talked to Douglas at the table about varieties of potatoes, and how pests could be controlled without using insecticides. Douglas was very keen on this. However, it did not look to his son's critical eye that Mr Lochlan was actually doing any more work.

But now, Finn did not want to waste time talking about Corumbeg. Grabbing this unexpected opportunity, he leaned forward and said, 'Douglas, tell me about Hirsay.'

Douglas was coming down the slip-road onto the motorway. He waited until he had edged out safely into the stream of traffic, then, settling down to drive comfortably in the inside lane, he said, 'Ah, yes. Hirsay. You've never been there?'

'No,' said Finn.

'Bess and I have, twice,' Douglas told him. 'The first time was years ago, before we were married, and went to Kenya. Then we went again, two summers ago. We saw an appeal in a geographical magazine for people to go and help rebuild the school. Mr Ackerley said that he would provide the materials, if volunteers would do the building work. After our first spell in Glasgow, we were dying to get away to a remote place again. So we went for three weeks, in July, while Chris went on holiday with his auntie. The weather was beautiful, which was lucky for us. It isn't always so.'

Finn knew this. 'Grandpa said the storms were terrific,' he said. 'Sometimes the spray from the sea came right over the roof of the cottage. Grandpa's father was drowned at sea in a sudden storm,' he added solemnly.

Douglas nodded. 'That must have happened all too often,' he said. He paused, then went on slowly, 'It's a strange place. As strange as any I've ever been in. Even on a warm summer day, you can sense what it would be like if the sun disappeared. There's something sinister about the way the sea sucks and spits around the rocks.

40

The wind never dies down, and its eerie whistling can really get on your nerves. All the time you feel there's darkness behind the light. It has something to do with those terrible black cliffs, I suppose. They're so brooding and oppressive.' Douglas's voice faded as he said this, but then strengthened again. 'I think,' he said, 'that what makes Hirsay so frightening – beautiful, magical but frightening – is the feeling that it can't be tamed. You know that people lived and died there, and that the last of them were swept away even as they tried desperately to cling on, but to Hirsay it's as if they'd never been. Not that it has forgotten them, but that it never noticed they were there. People are like butterflies on Hirsay, creatures of a day.'

Finn was not sure that he understood all this, or that he liked what he did understand. Certainly this sombre description did not match the picture of Hirsay which he carried in his mind, with hard-working but contented Islanders, and happy children to whom Hirsay was the most desirable home on earth. Grandpa had never suggested that it was frightening, except during the occasional storm – but then everyone had been cosy indoors, telling stories by the peat fire. Still, Finn didn't want to argue with Douglas, who could shrug and say, 'You haven't been there. I have.'

So, after he had sat for a few moments, looking out of the car window at distant mountains, he said, 'If what you say is true, why bother to rebuild the school?'

'Good point,' said Douglas approvingly. 'The answer is, because Hirsay matters to people. It's beautiful, challenging, terrifying. It gives us back something most of us have lost nowadays, a sense of wonder. Places like Hirsay may not need people, but people need places like Hirsay, and Alaska, and the Gobi

Desert, and Peru. As our world gets more and more like the centre of London, we need these places more and more.'

Finn left it at that. It was not what he had hoped to hear, but he liked the feeling that Douglas was treating him as an equal, and he intended to think over what he had said.

In Perth, they left the car in the municipal carpark, and walked along by the river Tay, watching as the breeze whisked the fast grey water. Finn tried to copy Douglas's long, easy stride, and thought how nice it was to have his new friend all to himself in this unexpected way. At a do-it-yourself store, they bought buckets of whitewash, rolls of wire netting and coils of thick, rustproof wire. The shopkeeper allowed them to bring the car round, and load it up outside the shop. Finn was packed in with the whitewash under his feet, and the rolls of wire netting almost resting on his shoulders. Then they were off home.

When they were clear of the town, and on the straight motorway again, Douglas said suddenly, 'Hey, Finn! Would you like to hear a story?'

'Yes, please,' replied Finn happily.

7 The Story of the Northern Star

Douglas's story began far away across the Atlantic Ocean, on the wild, rocky seaboard of Newfoundland. There, on tiny, windswept islands, and in crannies on sea-washed rocks, grew a little flower called *stella aquilonaris*, the Northern Star. In its natural habitat, it grew and multiplied like a weed, and when scientists at a Canadian university had discovered that a powerful drug could be made from its leaves, it had not occurred to them that the supply would ever be in danger.

It had seemed likely that the drug could be used to treat a number of crippling illnesses, and a small quantity of the plant had been flown to the laboratory in Glasgow where Douglas's wife Bess worked. Scientists there were researching along similar lines. Bess had been wildly excited, because she thought they were on the verge of a discovery which would help thousands of people so ill that their lives were hardly worth living. But when she wrote to the university in Canada to ask if her lab could have a further supply of the plant, the answer contained some appalling news.

'What was it?' demanded Finn. He had no idea why Douglas was telling him this story, but, like all Douglas's stories, it was very interesting to him.

'It was,' replied Douglas, so vehemently that Finn jumped, 'that a filthy great tanker had run aground on an island off the coast where the Northern Star grew, and leaked most of its poisonous oil into the sea. The wind and tide had spread it all over the rocks, and within three days, birds, seals and sea creatures were doomed. The only known habitat of the Northern Star was wiped out completely, in the worst marine pollution disaster the world has ever known.

'Something that would have given hope and relief to innocent, suffering people,' said Douglas, with a raw grief in his voice that made Finn wince, 'was stripped off the face of the earth by the greed and incompetence of their fellow human beings. Not only was the tanker overloaded, but it was unfit even to put to sea.'

The next silence was a long one, broken only by the hum of the engine, and the regular whoosh of other vehicles speeding past theirs. Eventually Finn dared to ask, 'Is that the end of the story?'

He was relieved when, in the rear-view mirror, he saw the deep creases around Douglas's eyes crinkle into a smile.

'No,' he replied. 'That's just half of it.'

'Now for the good news?' asked Finn hopefully.

'Possibly,' said Douglas. 'The professor in Canada who wrote to Bess said that they had a small amount of seed in their lab, but they weren't willing to share. They were finding it very slow to germinate in artificial conditions, and they didn't want to lose any. He said that if they could get the stuff to grow, they might share later on, but he wasn't going to make any promises. Bess and co were pretty choked, as you can imagine. But this is where the plot thickens.'

'How so?' asked Finn eagerly.

'Well,' said Douglas, 'it was like this. Not long afterwards, our Bess started saying she was sure she had

44

seen the stuff – *stella aquilonaris* – somewhere before. On and on she went about it, night and day. Where could it have been? It wasn't in the Botanic Gardens. She was sure of that. Could it have been in her Auntie Lizzie's garden at Dunoon when she was a little girl? Or in Nepal, or when we lived in Huancayo? Me and Chris were getting fed up with it. And then the blessed girl remembered. Three o'clock in the morning, poke, poke at my back. Did I remember climbing the Red Hill on Hirsay? Did I remember wee white flowers growing on the summit?'

And that was when Finn's heart gave a great, incredulous, exultant bound, because he remembered too.

'Pathan,' he cried.

'Eh?' said Douglas.

'*Pathan*,' squealed Finn, jumping up and down, and getting his jersey caught in the wire netting. 'That's what it's called, not stella thingummy-jig. I know, because Grandpa told me. It flowers all summer long, and it only grows on Hirsay, not on Skye, or Lewis, or any of these other islands. The Hirsay folk fed it to their sick cattle, and made medicine from it to take when they had coughs or sore stomachs. Women took it to help the pain when they were having babies, and my great-Granny made plasters with it to put on when Grandpa skinned his knee. It cured everything, Douglas, and it's called pathan.'

They had left the motorway, and driven all the way along the Glen Road as they talked. Now, as Douglas swung the car onto the track to Corumbeg, he was laughing gleefully.

'Is that not amazing?' he said. 'Well, whatever it's called, Bess and I are going to Hirsay in October to get some. We're going to plant our own seed, and make it grow. And when the stuff's rampaging all over our garden, are we going to share it with those sniffy Canadians? No way!'

8   Saturday

It was not surprising, after so much excitement, that Finn found it hard to sleep that night. His thoughts chased themselves round and round inside his head, refusing to settle.

For several nights past, he had been using the time between putting out the light and falling asleep to imagine Douglas into the Hirsay Story. This was pleasurable, because he could leave out all the things that displeased him in real life – notably the existence of Chris, and Douglas's boasting about him – and make Douglas the person Finn would have preferred him to be.

So far, in the story, Douglas was a wise, powerful and childless stranger, Dugald of the Mountains, who had come ashore from a small boat, met Jamie and Finn on the beach, and offered to help them in their fight against the pirates. After some amiable argument, Finn's idea of rowing out to the *Black Snake* in the dark, and firing her, had been accepted by the other two. Tonight, Finn meant to take the story on from there, perhaps to the point where Dugald, watching the pirate galleon burn, would reveal that he was the boys' long-lost uncle.

Unfortunately, the events of the afternoon had made it impossible for him to concentrate on this satisfying development. For the first time since he started playing his nocturnal game, the pull of reality was stronger than that of the story. No sooner had Finn composed a mind-picture of Dugald, Jamie and himself in the rowing-boat, with Dugald pulling on the muffled oars, than it disintegrated. His thoughts slipped away to the tale Douglas had told him in the car, of the healing plant that now grew nowhere in the world except on the Red Hill of Hirsay. Finn was not a person who had ever cared very much about the pain and distress of others; if there was a collection for a charity at school, he put the fifty pence Granny gave him in the box, but failed to listen when Mrs Ritchie was explaining why the money was needed.

But tonight he really did feel indignant about that vile oil tanker which had destroyed the Canadian shore where the Northern Star grew. He felt pity for the invalids whose hope of a cure had been snatched away by a disaster beyond the control of ordinary people, and he hoped passionately that the seeds from the Hirsay plant would grow in the Coopers' garden. Although he did not know it, this was an important point in his life. Infected by Douglas's warm-hearted concern, he was for the first time ever, feeling interested in happenings outside the imagined Island world.

Long after his father, Douglas and Granny had come up to bed, Finn was still awake, and when he did eventually fall asleep, it was to dream that he was on Hirsay. But he was alone, and this was not the summer Island where he and Jamie Lochlan lived so happily together. It was the Hirsay which Douglas had described in the car, and which Finn would have preferred not to acknowledge, with its black cliffs and hungry sea, and restless wind blowing darkness over the sun.

Because the next day was Saturday, Finn slept late, and when he did at last come downstairs, it was to discover that Douglas had gone off at first light to spend the day at home with Bess and Chris. He was peeved. It had never occurred to him that Douglas would have days off. After breakfast, he moped about in the yard, sullenly kicking a ball against the stable wall. Then he went upstairs, and painted a picture of the *Black Snake*, on fire in Sheep Sound.

Douglas arrived back at seven in the evening, full of the news that Chris had won a place in his school's swimming team. When he had made sure that everyone knew about this, and had had a cup of coffee, he went whistling upstairs to his room.

'He does think the world of that boy,' remarked Granny, rubbing it in.

Since she did not seem to expect a reply, Finn said nothing, and shortly afterwards went upstairs too. He had finishing touches to put to his painting, and thought he might then begin a portrait of the pirate captain, Ebenezer Blood. But the zest had gone out of the game.

The previous evening, thrilled because Douglas had shared his story of Hirsay and pathan, Finn had almost invited him into his room, and shown him the map of the Island, and the pictures he and Grandpa had made. But, embarrassed by the fairy-tale inventions now marked indelibly on the map, he had held back, and now he was glad. He was disgruntled because a whole day that he might have spent with Douglas had been wasted, unreasonably huffy because Douglas seemed to prefer the company at home to the company at Corumbeg, and sick to death of hearing about the marvellousness of Chris. Savagely, as he drew the Captain's hideous face, Finn hoped that Chris would slip, and fall in the swimming pool with all his clothes on. He hoped he'd fall in a snowdrift with his skis. He hoped everybody would laugh. And he vowed that he would not let Douglas see the map. The last thing he wanted was to be told that Chris could draw maps too.

It was a vow, however, no sooner made than it was broken. About two minutes later, Finn heard movement next door, then the sound of Douglas's feet on the landing. There was a tap on his door, and, for the first time ever, Douglas poked his shaggy head round the edge.

'Sorry to disturb you, Finn,' he said apologetically, 'but do you happen to have a pencil-sharpener handy?'

What happened then was inevitable. Finn opened his desk drawer, and scrabbled around among the junk it contained. When he had located a box of pencil-sharpeners, and raised his head, he saw that Douglas had come right in. With conflicting feelings of annoyance, pride and apprehension, Finn watched him looking intently at the map of Hirsay, and its wide border of neatly mounted drawings and paintings. His expression was impossible to read.

'Well?' snapped Finn at last, both challenging and defiant.

Douglas did not seem to notice his tone. He went on staring at the map, but shook his head uncertainly.

'I don't know,' he said at last. 'It's the most beautiful map I've ever seen. Amazing, really. Only —'

'Only what?'

'Only it's not what it's like.'

Finn was already in a bad mood, and now shock and confusion made him furious. For an ugly instant, he wanted to shout, 'So what? I never asked you to come in here. I didn't want you to look at it. It's private. Go away!' But he could never had spoken such words to Douglas, no matter how angry he was. Still, he could not keep the hurt and indignation out of his voice.

'It is what it's like,' he said. 'Grandpa drew the map. He knew what it was like, if anyone did.'

'Hang on,' said Douglas gently, seeing Finn's flushed face. 'I'm not insulting Grandpa. It's a wonderful map. There's the village, and the church, and the Pool of Seals, and Hamasgeir, the Ocean Rock. And there's the Red Hill, and the cliff top where Bess saw her Northern Star. But —' he pointed to Eilean nan Gall '— there's no island there, and there isn't a lighthouse either, or a fort on the Red Hill. And as for these pirates and Blue Men – I thought these kind of folk were only found in stories. It's not my business, of course, but – well, I just wonder whether this is how you think the Island is, or how you'd like it to be.'

This was terrible. Finn blushed to the roots of his thick fair hair.

'It's both,' he muttered. 'It's a game I play. There's nothing wrong with that, is there?'

'Nothing at all,' said Douglas, 'as long as you know the difference. I'm sorry I intruded.'

To his horror, Finn felt the sting of tears behind his eyes. Angrily, he forced them back.

'You didn't,' he said. 'I wanted – that is, I expect I'd have told you sometime. Do you want the aeroplane sharpener or the Mickey Mouse?'

Granny had been on her cocoa round, and Finn was in bed when Douglas reappeared. He sat down, greatly overlapping Finn's stool, and looked at him thoughtfully.

'I've had an idea,' he said.

Finn watched him from the pillow. He was very tired.

'Am I in the idea?' he asked.

'You are. I was thinking,' Douglas went on, 'that when we go to Hirsay in October, you might like to come with us. It will only be for a couple of days, just after I finish here, because Bess has had nearly all her leave for this year. But if you'd like to come and see what Grandpa's Island is really like, we'd love to have you along.'

At that moment, nothing could have prevented the great shout of joy which Finn's whole body seemed to give. But almost immediately, a cold splash of doubt fell on his heart.

'Oh, Douglas,' he whispered. 'Please. Only – what if Dad says no?'

'He says yes,' Douglas reassured him. 'I've just been down to his study to ask him.' For perhaps a minute, Finn's happiness was cloudless. Then Douglas got up to go.

'That's settled, then,' he said, grinning down at Finn. 'We'll have great fun, and it will be nice for Chris to have a chum to share a bedroom with.'

Chris, thought Finn, as the light went out.

9 An Unwelcome Guest

If anyone had told Finn that he could receive an invitation to visit Hirsay, and not be completely happy, he would have found it impossible to believe. It was, after all, a long dream suddenly come true. Yet scarcely had Douglas closed the door behind him before the first great experience of joy began to be soured, and overshadowed by discontent.

Finn did try hard to feel thrilled. Next morning, he crossed off the date on the calendar above his bed, beginning the conventional count-down to the Great Day when he would leave for Hirsay. And often, during the glowing September days that followed, he would close his eyes over the cider-gold hills and woods of Glenaire, to imagine himself arriving on the Island. He would land at the jetty, and see the church, and the school, and the walls of the cottage where Grandpa was born. He would walk to the graveyard, and stand in the place where his ancestors were buried. He would watch the white drift of sea birds, and seals basking on Hamasgeir.

But, being Finn, this was not dream enough for him. Soon the scene shifted, and he was imagining the newspaper arriving at Corumbeg, and Granny sitting down to read it by the fire.

'Good heavens,' she would say in amazement. 'Colin,

look at this.'

Then his father would lean forward to take the paper, and Finn would see a proud expression spread over his face as he read the headline,

HIRSAY BOY FINDS WONDER PLANT

and saw the close-up photograph of Finn, modestly holding up a sprig of pathan.

'Well done, my boy,' he would say, deeply impressed for the first time ever.

Only, it would not be like that. Because now it was a real story, and Finn was obliged to discard this gratifying version of events for another, much less to his taste. In it, it would not be Finn Lochlan, but Bess Cooper, a Glasgow scientist and traveller, who would get the credit for finding the pathan. Finn – if he were in the photograph at all – would have to share it with her, her husband Douglas, the renowned mountaineer, and their son, Chris.

It was at the recollection of this last name that Finn's mind darkened, and the colours of the world thinned. All his discontent was centred on Chris Cooper, who could swim and sail, and climb rocks and mountains, and had the good fortune to be Douglas's son. Whether he admitted it or not, Finn was bitterly jealous of the boy who could do, in real life, all the things he could only do in an imaginary one, and whose father was proud of him. Chris was the spoiler of Finn's world.

Perhaps the hardest thing of all was that, even in bed at night, Finn now found it impossible to escape into his life with young Jamie Lochlan, among the pirates and sinister Blue Men. Whenever he tried to find solace in that story, Chris Cooper appeared in his mind's eye, tall, dark, confident and clever, laughing at boys who played silly pirate games while he was climbing

54

mountains, and sailing across the Irish Sea. Finn was too confused to notice that Chris Cooper was as much a figure of his own imagination as young Jamie Lochlan was. He only knew that he didn't want to share Hirsay with him, or anything else. His sole consolation was that the trip to Hirsay was still some weeks away. He did not have to meet the boy wonder yet awhile.

Then something awful happened.

Douglas had only been at Corumbeg for three weeks, but to anyone who had known the place before, the difference he had made was astonishing. Barns had been whitewashed, and fences mended. Cages of wire netting had been constructed to protect the vegetable garden, and the hens, thriving on a new food-mix suggested by Douglas, were laying again. Eggs had actually been sold at Perth market.

But the greatest change was in the farmer himself. Somehow, Douglas seemed to have persuaded Mr Lochlan that if he really wanted to make a success of Corumbeg, he was going to have to stir himself, and do some hard work. So, perhaps rather to his own surprise, Mr Lochlan had rolled up his sleeves, taken up a whitewash brush, and gone out to the yard. Perhaps to his even greater surprise, he discovered that he was enjoying himself. On some days, he wrote no poetry at all.

Working alongside Douglas, Mr Lochlan mended fences, improved the henhouse, dug over the vegetable beds. His pale skin turned brown in the open air, his stooping shoulders lifted, and he began to have an air of self-esteem which he had never had before. And although he still snorted at Finn, and found no more to say to him than he ever had done, he laughed normally with Douglas, looking like a young man. Finn was aware of this transformation, and would have been intrigued, had he not been so preoccupied with his own affairs. What he could not miss was the expression in Granny's dark eyes as she looked at her son, tender, happy and amazed. It was as if she were seeing someone she had known and loved long ago, but had never expected to meet again.

So both Mr Lochlan and Granny were in the mood to do Douglas any favour they possibly could. What happened next was infuriating to Finn, but, in the circumstances, understandable.

On a Friday morning, when he had finished breakfast, Finn had gone upstairs to fetch his school bag, leaving his father, Granny and Douglas at the table. Since he had stopped working with Tam Orr, Douglas did not go out quite so early, and had breakfast with the family. When Finn came down again, he sat on the bottom step of the stair to put on his outdoor shoes, and that was when he heard the grown-ups' voices through the open kitchen door.

'Look, Douglas,' Granny was saying, 'it won't be any trouble. He can sleep on a camp-bed in Finn's room, and Mrs Ritchie won't mind having him at Yett School for a couple of weeks before the autumn holiday. It will be nice for the boys to get to know each other before you take them to Hirsay. Bring him back with you on Sunday night.'

Finn felt himself go rigid with shock and disbelief. His fingers fumbled with his lace, and his bottom seemed to freeze to the stair. He heard his father saying heartily, 'Good idea. You do that,' then Douglas sounding grateful.

'It's very good of you both. Bess arranged some time ago that her sister would come and look after Chris while she went to London on this course, but if the poor woman has shingles, then of course she can't come. Bess is quite prepared to stay at home, but she'd be delighted if she didn't have to. Thanks very much indeed.'

Finn made an effort, and got to his feet. Without saying goodbye, he walked through the kitchen into the yard, and climbed into the back of the Land-rover. It was panic, as much as rage, which made him feel as if a swarm of black insects was beating around his head.

There was, of course, nothing that could be done to change things. Finn knew that perfectly well. Douglas, who had saved up last week's day off so that he could have a weekend at home, had departed before Finn came back from school. Next time he appeared, he would have cocky Chris in tow. When Finn told Granny that he would rather not have Chris Cooper sharing his room, he got what he expected, one of her teachery tickings off.

'Don't be tiresome, Finn. We all owe Douglas a great deal, and you most of all. How do you think you would ever get to Hirsay, if he hadn't offered to take you? The least you can do in return is to be friendly to his little lad.'

Little lad, thought Finn glumly. Chris Cooper was a year older than he was, and was a man of Douglas Cooper's size likely to have a little lad? But he knew when Granny wasn't going to give in, and when he went into his room on Sunday afternoon, and found a camp-bed, neatly made up in the corner, he made no fuss.

The only remaining question was whether he ought to take down the map of Hirsay and his pictures, and hide them under his bed until the unwelcome guest had departed. He was strongly tempted to do so, because he hated the idea of Chris Cooper looking at the map, perhaps with a sneer on his dark, handsome face. On the other hand, Douglas was bound to come in to make sure that Chris was comfortable, and might be offended if he saw that Finn had taken the map down. Finn couldn't afford to annoy Douglas, who could withdraw the invitation to go to Hirsay. However unfriendly his feelings towards Chris might be, Finn still wanted to go to the Island, more than anything else in the world. So he left the map where it was.

10   Chris Cooper

Over the weekend, the weather continued fair, with sharp, dew-laden mornings and mellow, golden afternoons. After their usual weeks of hesitation, the trees in the valley were relinquishing their summer green for a more showy, russet dress, and the hedgerows were strung with scarlet rosehips and crimson haws. Granny shivered in the hard-edged, frosty evenings, but after lunch she would pull her basket chair to the yard door, and sit there in the sunshine, looking out at hills tinted topaz and mauve, under a pale blue wash of sky. Finn stayed in his room. If there was beauty in Glenaire, he wanted none of it.

It was a long weekend for Finn. He tried to while it away by drawing a series of pictures, showing the adventures of the Blue Men on their voyage to Hirsay from Spitzbergen, where they had a castle amid the snow. But his interest in these characters was fitful nowadays; he just couldn't live in the Hirsay Story in the way he used to do. Now he found it difficult to concentrate on anything except the approaching arrival of Chris Cooper, and there was a little spice of curiosity mixed with his fear. By Sunday afternoon, he felt that if it had to happen, it would be better to have it over, and when he looked at his watch and saw that it was almost half-past five, he felt something like relief. He went downstairs to the kitchen, and sat by the fire with a comic open in front of his face.

Granny had made a chocolate cake, and Douglas's favourite ham and egg pie. Mr Lochlan, who had recently taken to walking up the hill to peer at his sheep, came in and took off his coat and boots. While he warmed his behind at the fire, the minutes ticked on towards ten to six. The room began to darken, and Granny switched on the light.

'I hope they're not going to be late,' she said.

Finn was making a smart reply to this inside his own head, when he heard the sound of Douglas's car coming up the track, then the double hoot of his horn in the yard, announcing, 'We're here'. Granny hurried hospitably to the door, and Finn trailed after her. Standing at her back, he peeped out into the gauzy evening, and heard his own gasp of astonishment at what he saw. Last month, the biggest man Finn had ever seen had emerged from the blue Ford. Today, it seemed to be the turn of the smallest boy.

The smallest eleven year old, at least. Far from being a dark, handsome replica of his father, the real Chris Cooper was tiny, more than a head shorter than Finn, who was just ten. He had spiky brown hair, a pouting mouth, and grey eyes in a pale, pointed face. Very thin in his blue tracksuit, he stood beside his father, hanging on determinedly to Shep's collar, so that the dog could not run to greet Finn. No words were needed to assure Finn that Chris was no more delighted to see him than he was to see Chris.

With typical provokingness, the grown-ups thrust them towards each other.

'Look, Chris. Here's Finn. Say hello.' That was Douglas.

'Come away in out of the cold, Chris. Finn will take you upstairs, and show you where you're going to sleep. Help Chris with his bag, Finn.' That was Granny.

'Come on, you two. Try a smile.' That was Mr Lochlan, and coming from him, it was breathtaking.

To get away from them, Finn lifted Chris's blue nylon bag, and said, 'Follow me.' He walked across the kitchen towards the hall, aware of the other boy's reluctant shuffle behind him. Upstairs, Finn said things like, 'You're in here with me,' and, 'This is the bathroom.' He did not receive so much as a grunt in reply.

All through supper, Chris sat with his eyes fixed on his plate, while Finn stared at him in astonishment. Obviously this was not the robust, confident, athletic Chris of his jealous imagining, but could he possibly be the boy who had climbed Ben Nevis, sailed to Ireland, and cycled from Glasgow to Inverness? Finn let his eyes slide along to Douglas, who was pointedly ignoring Chris, and discussing the market price of sows with Mr Lochlan. Could Douglas have been lying? The idea was preposterous. Yet there was a strained, unhappy look about his eyes which Finn had never seen before. Presumably there had been a row in the car.

When the meal was over, Douglas said, 'Get your jacket, Chris, and we'll take Shep out.' He did not ask Finn to accompany them, and Finn had no desire to do so. He wanted to stay with Granny, and discuss Chris Cooper's extraordinary behaviour. But although he cleared the table, and dried all the dishes for her, all Finn could get her to say was, 'You must be kind to him, Finn. Poor little boy.'

11   Trouble at Yett School

In the morning, it was Douglas who took the two boys down to school. He said he wanted to have a word with Mrs Ritchie, which didn't surprise Finn. He wondered whether Douglas wanted to explain to her that Chris had lost his tongue. Last night, when Finn had gone upstairs, he had found Chris already in the camp-bed, facing the wall, and with the bedclothes pulled up over his head. This morning, Chris had got up, come downstairs and eaten his breakfast in total silence. Now he was sitting in the back of the car beside Finn, wearing grey trousers and a red sweatshirt, and looking as if he had swallowed a lemon.

All the way down to Yett, Chris stared moodily out of the window, and Finn, who had nothing he wanted to say either, sat slumped in the opposite corner, reading a comic. Even Douglas, normally so chatty, gave up after, 'Look, Chris, a weasel!' and, 'Do you see that pheasant in the field?' had met with no response. Only when they reached the school gate did he speak again. 'Go with Finn, Chris,' he said, kindly but firmly. 'I'll go and speak to Mrs Ritchie now. You'll get on fine, you'll see.'

He opened the door to let the boys out, then strode away across the playground, disappearing through the green door. Finn was very thankful that at this moment, the bell rang, and they had to stand in the line.

Mrs Ritchie talked to Douglas in the corridor for a few minutes, then came into the classroom. She gave Chris a chair at Finn's table, but not next to Finn.

'Have a look at the pictures on the wall,' she told him, 'then take a book from the Library Corner. When I've got the others started, I'll give you some work to do.'

While he was copying down his assignment of work from the blackboard, Finn was aware of Chris slouching around the perimeter of the room, glancing unenthusiastically at a mural of Yett village, and paintings of Mary, Queen of Scots visiting Yett Tower. After a very short time he returned to his chair with a thick, unillustrated book, and sat staring fixedly at the first page. Meanwhile, Mrs Ritchie visited all the tables, explaining to the groups what she wanted them to do. This took a while, but eventually she returned to her desk and said, 'Come to me now, Chris, please.'

Finn, who was supposed to be doing Maths, watched Chris creeping out, and wished the buzz of talk around him would subside, so that he could hear what Mrs Ritchie was saying to him. He could see her round head with its black bun nodding as she spoke, and presently Chris returned, carrying a text-book and an exercise-book. Finn watched him prop up the text-book as a screen, and cup his left hand furtively, to hide what he was writing. He sat, biting his lip and getting redder about the ears, until Mrs Ritchie called him out again. He stood at her side, looking sullen, while she talked to him about what he had written.

Of all the strong emotions Chris Cooper had aroused in Finn, curiosity was the only one left, and now it got the better of him. Lifting his book, he walked out to

Mrs Ritchie's desk.

'What is it, Finn?'

'Please, I'm not sure how to do number four.'

'Then try number five, and I'll help you when I've finished helping Chris.'

Scarcely able to believe what he had seen, Finn returned to his seat. He had only been out of it for half a minute, but that had been long enough to squint at Chris's exercise-book. The boy had spent twenty minutes writing three and a half lines. His handwriting was like a six-year-old's, and hardly a word was correctly spelt. A sudden wave of decent pity swept over Finn. Poor little devil, he thought. No wonder he hadn't wanted to come to Corumbeg.

The rest of the morning was terrible. Chris did reasonably well at Maths, and he could solve a puzzle on the computer. But he couldn't write a story, and it soon became clear that he couldn't read. Finn wondered why Mrs Ritchie, who was a kindly woman, didn't just leave him to draw in a corner. He couldn't know that Douglas had asked her not to do this. The expression of misery on Chris's face upset Finn, but when, after lunch, he asked Chris to come and help with a dam which the children were building on the river Aire, behind the school, the response was venomous.

'Push off, Fish-face. I don't want to know you, and I don't want to play with you, and I don't want you feeling sorry for me. So do me a favour. Get lost.'

No one had ever called Finn 'Fish-face' before, and he was not pleased. But he didn't retaliate, and he didn't go down to the river with the other children. For Douglas's sake, he thought he should stick around, so he went and read his comic at the other end of the shelter from where Chris sat huddled on the bench. Then Chris went and locked himself in the lavatory.

The afternoon, when they watched television and went to Physical Education, was not so bad. No one could have said that Chris cheered up, but he looked less likely to scream and bolt from the room. Finn sensed that most of the children were very sympathetic, and he hoped that they would get through to going-home time without anything else happening to upset Chris. But it was not to be.

They were in the cloakroom, putting on their coats, when a malicious, sneering voice was heard by everybody. 'Hey, you, Finn Lochlan. Who's your stupid wee friend?'

'Shut your face, Aldie,' said Finn violently, and there were exclamations of disapproval from the other children.

'Yeah. Shut up, Andy.'

'Stow it, will you?'

'Pay no attention, Chris. He's a pig to everybody.'

'Never noticed you were so brilliant, Aldie.'

But Chris had had enough. Grabbing his bag, he fled from the school, raced across the playground, and flung himself into the back of the car. When Finn, angry and red-faced, caught up with him, it was in time to hear him wail, 'It's your fault, Dad. Mum should have stayed at home with me. I hate new schools.'

Then he burst into tears.

Chris's tormentor was called Andrew Aldie, and he was indeed a pig to everybody. He was bigger than the other children, with a round pink face, small blue eyes, and hair like ginger candy-floss. It was rumoured that his father was rich. Finn had never liked him, but during the next few days his dislike swelled to hatred such as he had never before felt for anyone. Andrew Aldie could not pass Chris's chair without hissing, 'Stupid!' and in the playground he kept up an endless stream of taunts.

'Hi, twit. Read any baby books today? Learned your ABC yet? D'you know how to spell moron?'

Chris, who still spoke to no one at school, and only Granny at home, pretended he didn't hear. There was nothing else he could do. His tormentor was twice his size.

Finn stood it until Thursday lunch-time, then, when Andrew Aldie came lurching over to the shelter to inquire whether Chris's father and mother were morons too, something snapped inside him. Closing his fist, he did what he had wanted to do for two years, and swung it hard into Andrew Aldie's face. The flow of blood was considerable.

And so, of course, was the fuss. Andrew's howls, loud enough to be heard at Perth, summoned Mrs Ritchie, who sent him off to Miss Barry to be cleaned up. Finn was ordered to go and stand at the classroom door. He went expecting trouble, but didn't care. Before Mrs Ritchie got to him, however, she had been stopped by the other children, and indignantly told the story of Chris Cooper's persecution.

'You can't blame Finn, Mrs Ritchie. Chris is his friend, after all.'

This would have been news to Finn, but Mrs Ritchie must have agreed. Finn got a fairly feeble, ritual ticking off, along lines of, 'You ought to have told me, and let me handle it. You must never do such a thing again.' Finn said that he wouldn't, but secretly he was very glad that he hadn't let her handle it. Teachers were not allowed to punch bullies on the nose. He was sent away, and Andrew Aldie was summoned to Mrs Ritchie.

In the afternoon, Chris folded a small piece of paper, and flicked it along the table to where Finn sat. Finn swept it off onto his knee, and opened it under the table. Written in large letters were the words, 'thanks Fin'. Finn grinned at Chris, and made the 'thumbs up' sign.

12   Finn has an Idea

That night in bed, the boys talked as if they had to make up for four wasted days. Sitting up and warming their hands on their mugs of cocoa, they gloated cosily over the defeat of Andrew Aldie, who had gone home snivelling and discomfited at half-past three. In the afternoon, Mrs Ritchie had had a great deal to say about people who were unkind to other people, and it was clear that Chris would have no more social problems during his visit to Yett School. His work problem would not go away so easily, as he explained ruefully to Finn.

'I never went to school at all until we left Huancayo, in Peru, when I was seven,' he said. 'Mum and Dad were supposed to teach me, but they were always away climbing mountains and taking photographs of gruesome flowers. They seemed to think that I'd pick up reading and writing the way I picked up Spanish, but I didn't, and in the next two years I went to eight different schools, which didn't help. That's why I cut up rough at the weekend. I hate changing schools.'

Finn could understand this. He had only changed once, and that was bad enough.

'What's your school in Glasgow like?' he asked.

'All right, I suppose,' said Chris indifferently. 'The kids there think I'm stupid too, but there isn't anybody as bad as that Aldie, thank heaven. I go to a remedial teacher three times a week, but I'm in a big class, and I just get further and further behind. And now that Mum and Dad have realised how hopeless I am, they're in an awful state about it, which makes it worse. Being so wee doesn't help, either.'

'I was surprised when I saw you,' admitted Finn. 'I thought you'd be like your Dad.'

Chris grinned, and it went through Finn's mind that a grin improved his face no end.

'Like a baby elephant, you mean?' he said. 'Just wait till you see my Mum. She says when she was my age, they used her as a bookmark. I'm like the bookmark side of the family.'

It was lightly said, but Finn knew it must be no joke, being half the size of everybody else in your class.

'Anyway, your Dad thinks you're marvellous,' he told Chris, wanting to say something heartening. 'He's never done telling us all the smart things you can do. I was getting fed up with it, actually.'

Chris squirmed down under the bed-clothes, and groaned comically.

'I'll bet,' he said. 'Auntie Pat gets fed up with it too. She keeps asking him if he knows how daft he sounds. And I get fed up with it myself. You see, these things – climbing and sailing and cycling – are only important to Dad because of what I can't do. If my school work was normal, he'd stop making a silly ass of himself, boasting about things that don't really matter.'

Finn was startled by this speech. He had thought of Douglas for so long as a perfect father that it was a shock to realise that he might make a fool of himself like ordinary fathers. Finn pulled his quilt up to his chin, and looked thoughtfully at Chris over the edge.

'So, don't you enjoy these things?' he asked.

Chris wrinkled up his nose, then blew out his cheeks.

'I suppose they're OK,' he said. 'I don't enjoy them the way Mum and Dad enjoy them. They think it isn't Saturday unless you climb a mountain. And,' he added, going pink at the recollection of an outrage, 'I draw the line at having to spend Christmas Day camping in the snow on Rannoch Moor. That was when I thought they'd really gone bananas. I want Santa Claus, and Christmas dinner in my own house, like other kids.'

He sounded so annoyed that Finn said uncertainly, 'Then – don't you like your mum and dad?'

But this question just made Chris burst out laughing. 'Oh, I like them, all right,' he said. 'They never let me stop them doing anything they want to do, they've messed up my education, and they think they're doing me a favour every time they take me up a gully in a force nine gale. But I can't help liking them. They never talk down to me, and they're kind and generous, and very funny. If they've got faults – well, show me the grown-up who hasn't. Hey, Finn, do you know what I'd really like to be?'

'No. What?'

'Your Granny's cat. I'd sit on her knee in front of the fire, and when she said, "Pussy-pussy-pussy", I'd say, "Mia-a-aou!"'

This made Finn laugh, but it also made it easier for him to share with Chris something he'd been thinking about a lot, but wouldn't have dared mention before. He waited until they had cleaned their teeth and been to the loo, then, when the light was out, he said into the darkness, 'Chris.'

'Mmm?'

'I bet my Granny could teach you to read.'

There was a long silence, during which Finn held his

breath. Perhaps Chris had heard this sort of thing too often. Perhaps he would be angry, and snarl a refusal. But, eventually, he said cautiously, 'What makes you think so?'

'Because,' said Finn, 'she taught Grandpa.' It was an old story, often proudly repeated, but Finn gladly told it again.

'Grandpa couldn't read or write when he married Granny. You see, when he was a boy on Hirsay, he hardly ever went to school. The teachers who came out to the Island never stayed for long, and often for months and months there were no lessons at all. When Grandpa came to Glasgow, he had to go to school for two years, but because he couldn't read and write, he didn't learn much there either. When he was fourteen, he was apprenticed to a gardener at a big house in the West End, and he was a gardener all his life, but he always wanted to be able to read and write. When he met Granny, she said she would teach him.'

'And did she?' asked Chris.

'Yes. It was hard work for both of them, but she did. And I reckon if she could teach a grown man to read, she could teach you.' There was another silence, then the objections began.

'Maybe your Grandpa was brighter than me.'

'No reason to think that,' countered Finn.

'I'm only here for another week.'

'You could stay longer.'

'Your Granny's old now. Maybe she couldn't be bothered.'

'Shall we ask her tomorrow, and see?'

Silence again. Then, 'I'll think about it,' Chris said.

Soon afterwards, he fell asleep, but Finn lay awake in the darkness, thinking about Grandpa. Since the old man had died, he had shrunk from the pain of remembering him directly, preferring to think of him as young Jamie Lochlan, the perfect boy of Hirsay. But now, disturbed by four days of watching Chris enduring hell in school, Finn could not prevent himself from wondering whether Grandpa had suffered similar agony when he had gone to school in Glasgow. Grandpa had been very small too – according to Granny, because the poor diet on Hirsay had stunted his growth. Finn didn't believe that, but – the question wouldn't go away. Had Grandpa been humiliated in class, perhaps tormented by an oversized thug like Andrew Aldie? It seemed only too likely, and it made Finn sick to think of it. Writhing uneasily in the darkness, he tried to turn his mind to something else, but always the Grandpa he had known came back to him, small, white-haired, mild of manner, with the sea in his blue eyes.

And something else was troubling Finn, something in the familiar story which suddenly seemed not quite right. Only gradually, he edged towards realising what it was. Grandpa had often told Finn that not having to go to school was one of the great benefits of living on Hirsay. It had been a joke between them. But, Finn now wondered, had he really believed it? Was the truth not that lack of early education had spoiled his life? He had certainly cared enough about his own illiteracy to get his wife to teach him, and he had made sure that his children got the best education available. Finn's father had gone to Glasgow University, and Auntie Phyllis had gone to Cambridge. What Grandpa had said, and what he had done, didn't quite fit.

For the first time ever, Finn was on the verge of admitting that there might have been one drawback to living on Hirsay, and that Grandpa might have been –

not lying, of course, but perhaps not telling the whole truth. But he was not ready for that. Recently, real events and people had become more important to him than the imaginary ones of the Hirsay Story, but Hirsay was still at the centre of his world. If he allowed himself to doubt Grandpa's version of life on the Island, that world would fall apart.

So he shelved the problem, and fell asleep.

13   Friendships

Next afternoon, Finn and Chris arrived home from school with a pleasant Friday feeling. Chris, who had had a good day and wanted to tell Douglas about it, would have dumped his bag and gone straight out to the steading to find him. But Finn had other ideas.

'We'll have a cup of tea with Granny first,' he said. 'She's been baking butterscotch cookies. I could smell them halfway up the hill.'

Chris could smell them too, and he willingly followed Finn into the warm, firelit kitchen. Granny had the teacups laid out on the table, and the cookies cooling on a wire-mesh tray.

Since the weekend, the weather had changed, and outside the day was chilly, and thinly grey. Finn would have been perfectly happy to sit on by the fire, telling Granny the news of school. Andrew Aldie had not turned up that morning. His little brother said he had a cold, but it was the general opinion in Mrs Ritchie's class that he didn't want to be seen with a bandage on his nose. However, the news would have to wait. As soon as he had finished his tea, Finn got up, and said firmly, 'Chris has something to ask you, Granny.'

'Have I?' asked Chris nervously.

'You know you have,' Finn told him, and departed upstairs. He gave them ten minutes, then came down again. 'Well?' he said.

He saw at once, with relief, that Chris had found courage to ask the vital question. He was standing beside Granny, leaning on the table, and looking anxiously into her long, handsome old face. She was holding her teacup in thin, veined hands, and was looking thoughtful. She turned her dark eyes on Finn and said, 'This was your idea, was it? Yes, I see why. But I couldn't teach anyone to read in a week, Finn. It just isn't possible.'

'He could stay for the autumn holiday,' pointed out Finn. 'It starts next Friday, and we have a fortnight.'

'I hope he will stay, if he'd like to,' replied Granny. 'But I couldn't teach him to read in three weeks either.'

'But you could teach him to read?' persisted Finn.

'Oh, yes, of course I could,' said Granny calmly. 'Most people who can't read, could. They just haven't had the right conditions for learning. Then they stop believing in themselves. There's no mystery about it.'

'Then please, could you start?' asked Chris.

There was a note of desperation in the boy's voice which made the old lady turn her head, and look at him closely. If she had been wavering, she now made up her mind.

'Listen,' she said. I'll have a word with your dad tonight, and if he and mum will let us keep you over the holidays, you and I shall spend some time together. As you say, we can make a start, and then we'll just have to see what happens after that.'

She rose and began to gather up the teacups, and the boys went out to play with Shep in the yard.

The next three weeks were the happiest Finn had spent

since Grandpa died. As the end of school slipped into the holiday, the good weather kindly returned. Summer seemed determined not to lose its grip until the last possible moment. Misty mornings and cold, moon-sharp nights bracketed days when warmth, and clear skies, contradicted the signs of autumn on every tree and hedge. Finn and Chris, at Douglas's command, fed the pigs, helped with the potato harvest and searched for eggs in the henhouse, fending off indignant henny attacks among the straw.

'Isn't this marvellous?' Chris kept saying. 'Isn't this a brill place, Finn?'

And sometimes Finn almost agreed, and then had to remind himself sternly that he really hated Corumbeg, and longed to be on an Island far away, under an intenser sky.

Douglas was overjoyed by Granny's suggestion that she might teach Chris, and after speaking to Bess on the telephone, had gladly agreed that Chris should stay at Corumbeg over the holiday. Granny had given him the same warning as she had given Finn, 'I can't teach him to read in three weeks,' but Douglas, like Chris, was prepared to settle for a start being made.

'Bess and I are to blame for this,' he admitted ashamedly. 'We were so absorbed in our own affairs that we didn't pay enough attention to what was happening, and now we can't forgive ourselves. If you would help Chris, I can't tell you how grateful we'd be.'

Granny waved her hand, and made a dismissive sound.

'My dear boy,' she said, 'it will be a pleasure. After all you've done for Colin, it's the least I can do.'

Finn, who had positioned himself where he could listen to this conversation, heard Douglas's deep laugh as he replied, 'Colin's fine now. All he needed was a bit of confidence. Has he told you he's going to get a dog, and send Tam Orr packing in the spring?'

'I'm glad to hear it,' said Granny, no doubt thinking of her balance at the Bank.

Finn went upstairs glowing with pleasure. Gruach, he thought excitedly. We'll call the dog Gruach. That was the name of the dog Grandpa had on the Island, when he was a little boy.

Each day after lunch, Granny and Chris went away to her room, while Finn did the washing-up. Neither of them said how they were getting on, but sometimes when he passed Granny's door, Finn could hear them laughing. And he noticed that Granny complained less about her rheumatism, and the draughts, and the general awfulness of everything at Corumbeg.

Meanwhile, there was plenty of time for fun. Finn need not have dreaded Chris's seeing his Hirsay map, because Chris was not interested in Hirsay. When he got around to looking at the map, he simply said, 'Oh, great. Pirates and Blue Men. Let's play.'

So, with Douglas's help, a pirate ship was built of scrap wood behind the barn, and the boys played there every day, fighting with wooden swords, and making each other walk the plank into the pigsty. Shep played too, leaping and barking like an excited puppy. Tam Orr said sourly that Shep would never make a sheepdog, because he didn't know whether he was a working animal or a family pet. Douglas was ruefully beginning to agree with him.

When the boys were not being pirates, they became Blue Men, whooping about in the heather, and jumping out on Douglas and Mr Lochlan from behind the wall. Mr Lochlan took this in reasonably good part. Finn reckoned he was only half as twitchy as he used to be, and although they didn't talk any more than usual, their bed-time sessions were less apologetic. And although Finn was secretly in fits of mirth at the sight of his father strutting with a shepherd's crook, he was generally more tolerant of him. This had something to do with Chris's assurance that no grown-up was faultless. If even Douglas Cooper could sometimes make an ass of himself, you had to make allowances for Colin Lochlan.

If Finn had only been able to extend this wise perception to include Grandpa, a lot of the troubles ahead of him might have been avoided. But Grandpa, who was dead, remained on a different plane. The old, night-time Hirsay Story, however, finally lost its intense significance, and became a merry game, played by two boys on an inland farm.

The middle weekend of the holiday, Bess came to stay, bringing lollipops, and warm woolly jerseys which she had bought in London for the boys to wear on Hirsay. She was a tiny, bright-eyed woman of thirty-five, with the same short, spiky brown hair as Chris, and a good-humoured, prematurely lined face. She too had lived out-of-doors in all weathers. Bess and Granny quickly became very friendly, and spent a lot of time leaning their elbows on the kitchen table, drinking tea and putting the world to rights. Bess called Granny 'Frances', which surprised Finn, who had forgotten she had any name except 'Granny'.

Bess was eagerly looking forward to her trip to Hirsay, and she was fascinated by what Finn could tell her about pathan. Feeling important, he fetched down a pencil drawing which Grandpa had made of the plant, and put it in front of her on the checked tablecloth.

'That's it, without a doubt,' said Bess happily. 'Did your Grandpa really say the Islanders used it as a medication, Finn?'

'Yes,' Finn assured her. 'They fed it to the cows to improve their milk, and they took it themselves for sore throats, stomach upsets, fever, rashes – you name it. Oh, and they made ointment from it, to rub on cuts and bruises. They got plenty of those, climbing cliffs to snare birds and collect the gannets' eggs. They thought it was magic. That was why they carried sprigs of it in their pockets. It was supposed to keep you safe from harm – a kind of lucky charm, you know.' Bess nodded her neat head.

'Yes, of course,' she said. 'It's the usual primitive mixing up of the scientific and the unscientific. What interests me most is that it was thought to cure such a wide range of ills, because that's what our experiments are suggesting too. And goodness knows,' she added, running her fingers through her hair, 'it does seem like magic – birds flying the Atlantic from Newfoundland, with seeds sticking to their beaks, giving us a new supply. And just when we thought all hope was lost. I can scarcely believe my luck.'

Finn considered this. Then, 'How d'you know the seeds came from Newfoundland to Hirsay?' he demanded. 'Why not Hirsay birds flying with seeds to Newfoundland?'

Bess looked startled, but then she grinned at him. 'I must admit I never thought of that,' she said.

On the last day of the holiday, Chris had to go home, and the sight of his sad little face looking out of the rear window of Bess's Mini, as it went down the hill, distressed everyone who was left behind. Finn could see that Granny was almost as upset as Chris was. The reading lessons were just beginning to go really well, and she was miserable about losing her pupil.

Finn's feelings were very mixed. He hated to see Chris go, and he knew that he was going to miss him terribly. But knowing that the long-wished-for visit to Hirsay was only a week away, and that Chris would be his companion there, made it hard for him to be really downcast. He could scarcely believe that once he had been so reluctant to share the Island with Chris. Now he couldn't imagine going there without him.

Finn refused to allow himself to dwell on the thought that when he returned, Douglas too would depart, and the three Lochlans would return to the lonely life they had led before he came. That would have to be faced, but not now. Now the Island was Finn's goal. He would not think beyond the Island.

14 Journey

On Thursday, the twenty-second of October, Finn crossed off the date on the calendar in his bedroom for the last time. Tomorrow, he would set out on his pilgrimage.

He had had his packing done since Sunday night, when, at a loose end without Chris, he had put into his rucksack all the things Bess had told him he would need on Hirsay. An extra pair of trousers, thick socks, shirts, pyjamas, the green oiled-wool jersey which she had given him.

'We must prepare for cold, and hope it will be warm,' Bess had said cheerfully. 'It's late in the year for island jaunting, but it really has to be now, when the seed-pods will be on the pathan. And our fisherman friend, Dan, says a storm isn't likely before mid-November, thank goodness.'

Finn noticed that Bess always used the Hirsay word, 'pathan', now, instead of the Latin *stella aquilonaris*. It was one of the things he liked her for.

One day after school, Douglas had taken Finn to Perth to buy a waterproof jacket and walking boots, advance Christmas presents from Granny. Finn had been wearing the boots a lot to break them in, and because he didn't want any of his things to look too new.

At half-past ten on Friday morning, a delighted Chris came tumbling out of the red Mini, hugged Granny, and dragged her off to her room for a quick reading lesson. Then, after lunch, Douglas put the roof-rack on the Ford, and piled it high with rucksacks, bundles of blankets and boxes of provisions. Bess said there was a stove in the old school, but she wasn't inclined to do a lot of cooking. So they had tins of ham and baked beans, instant soup and coffee, and pre-packed pies.

'Of course,' Finn told her airily, 'we could climb the cliffs and collect gannets' eggs. That's what they did in Grandpa's time.'

'You haven't seen the cliffs,' said Bess with a shudder. 'You'll have tinned ham and like it, Finn Lochlan.'

Finn knelt on the back seat as the car went down the hill, watching his father, Granny, and Shep, who was staying behind, recede into the distance. He thought that Mr Lochlan, standing at the gate in breeches and a checked shirt, with his hand on Shep's collar, really looked like a farmer now. Everyone at Corumbeg had been changed by the friendship of the Coopers, but the most obvious change was in Mr Lochlan.

The drive to the sea at Oban, through tawny mountain glens and by shining lochs, was beautiful, despite the appearance of puffy grey clouds to the west, suggesting a change in the weather. But Finn was blind to the view, and really to everything else as well. Although he read the comics which Douglas had provided, and played pocket chess with Chris in the back of the car, today was only a piece of time which he had to live through for the sake of tomorrow. All he could think of was that after this four-hour journey, and a seven-hour sail, he would be on Hirsay. He had always supposed that when this day came, he would be madly excited, but he wasn't. He just felt happy and expectant, as you do when you are nearing home.

It was six o'clock when they arrived in Oban, and went to a café overlooking the Bay to have something to eat.

'You'd better enjoy the fish and chips,' Bess told the boys. 'They're the last you'll see till you get back.'

'We could have fish,' pointed out Finn. 'Grandpa used to fish from Hamasgeir.'

Bess shook her head. 'No fishing,' she said. 'No falling in the sea and getting drowned. All right?'

Finn studied her as he spread butter on a slice of bread. Certainly she was very small, but for a person who had lived in such wild places, she seemed to him oddly timid about the challenge of Hirsay. But he didn't want to have an argument with her, so he tried to make his reply sound like a joke.

'Oh, come on, Bess. No climbing cliffs for eggs. No fishing. No getting drowned. What are we supposed to do for entertainment?'

It came out sounding cheekier than he had intended, but it wasn't that Bess seemed to mind. She sat twisting her wedding ring round her finger, looking back at him with serious eyes.

'Listen, Finn,' she said eventually. 'It isn't a laughing matter. I've been around a lot, and I'm not easily frightened. But you can take it from me. Hirsay is dangerous. You don't take risks in places like that. OK?'

Finn backed down reluctantly.

'OK,' he said.

When they had finished eating, Douglas paid the bill, and they drove down to the harbour. At the North Pier they unloaded the car, and went on board the fishing boat *Harebell*. Douglas's friend Dan, who was the skipper, took them below, and showed them the tiny, fishy-smelling cabin where they were to sleep. There were four bunks, two either side of a narrow passage, which Douglas blocked whichever way he stood. When it had been agreed, that in the interest of safety, the small skinny people should sleep on top, they went up on deck, glad to get out into the fresh air.

Night was falling as the vessel prepared to sail, and Finn leaned contentedly on the rail as the *Harebell* left harbour, and slipped gently down the Firth of Lorn. To port, he could see the twinkling lights of Seil Island, and the mountains of Mull rolling on the starboard side. The salt wind from the sea lifted his hair, and he could almost hear the call of Hirsay on its breath.

The fishermen were moving nimbly about the deck, preparing their nets for the night's fishing. But presently Dan came to join his passengers, a spare, wrinkled man in a blue jersey and a woolly hat. Chris had gone below to look at a comic in his bunk, but Finn stayed where he was, watching the pale turquoise swathe which the bows cut in the dark water, and listening with half an ear to the conversation of the grown-ups. Most of it was about places and people unknown to him, but when Hirsay was mentioned, his ears naturally pricked up.

It was Dan who was speaking, in the soft, precise voice of the Highlands. 'It is as well you did not come to Hirsay a fortnight ago, Douglas. Dear me, no. A great crowd of hooligans they were, the people who were on the Island then.'

Douglas sounded very surprised.

'A fortnight ago?' he repeated. 'I didn't think anyone came to Hirsay as late as October, unless they had a special reason, like us. Well, well. Do you suppose Mr

Ackerley knew they were there?'

'I am certain he did not,' said Dan, disapprovingly. 'Not his kind of person at all. Several nights, when we were fishing nearby, we heard them shouting and singing – blind drunk, they sounded to be. And they had lit bonfires, you could see from miles out to sea. I'm hoping you will have no terrible mess to clear up at the school, when you get there.'

'How many of them?' asked Bess, frowning.

Dan shrugged his bony shoulders. 'I could not say. Twelve, perhaps. There was a large motor yacht tied up at the jetty for four or five days.'

His tone told them all exactly what he thought of large motor yachts.

Finn felt anxious and indignant as he went below, but he fell asleep quite quickly in his lower bunk. As the *Harebell*'s softly throbbing engine drove her forward into the Atlantic, he slept dreamlessly. Yet he scarcely felt he had slept at all when, in the darkness, he felt a hand on his shoulder, and heard Douglas's voice whisper, 'Finn! Come and see.' With his eyes half shut, he got out of his bunk, and felt a blanket being placed around his shoulders, over his pyjamas.

Then Douglas steered him out of the cabin, and up the steep ladder to the deck, where the fishermen were intent on emptying their net of its burden of shining fish. But Douglas drew Finn up over coils of rope into the bows, and in the fragile lilac dawn he saw the Island, black and far away, crouching like a great beast against the sky.

15 Finn's Island

During the next hour, the Island slowly grew in size, lightening to pallid green under a low grey sky. Then, as the *Harebell* drew near, suddenly it revealed its true colours, black for the tumbled rocks that lay like ruined walls along the sea's edge, green and fawn for the stony lower slopes, wine for the Red Hill. As Hirsay rushed upon him in the expected blizzard of birds, Finn stood proudly in the bows with Chris, pointing out landmarks which were as familiar as if he had seen them every day of his life.

'That's Hamasgeir, the Ocean Rock. And there, on the left – that's the inlet called the Pool of Seals. There's the church, and – oh, look. I think I can see the wall of the graveyard, behind the school.'

The black water slapped against the little concrete jetty as the *Harebell* came alongside, and the gulls watched speculatively as the Island four unloaded their belongings. Dan, who was in a hurry to be off back to Oban with his catch, did not offer them assistance.

'We shall be here for you on Monday morning, Douglas,' he called, as the boat slid out into the Bay again. 'See you are ready in good time, so that we do not miss the tide.'

They waved, and the fishermen waved back, then they hoisted their gear, and set out along the rough stone causeway which connected the jetty with the village. Finn knew that the causeway was never dry; even at low tide, the sea was not very far away. Chris grumbled about the weight of his rucksack, but Finn walked in a dream, listening to the sea and the white birds crying, tasting the salt on his lips, seeing ahead of him the swift upward sweep of the Red Hill.

The old school, painted white and roofed with new slates, stood at right angles to Mr Ackerley's long, low house, where the Island minister had lived long ago. Douglas went to fetch the key from a hole in the wall of the ruined church, while Bess, Finn and Chris waited on the doorstep, drawing their jackets more closely round them. Finn was glad of the warm jersey Bess had given him, as the wind was indeed cold.

Inside, the old schoolroom had been partitioned to make three smaller rooms. At the back, there was a kitchen with a long table and chairs, as well as a bottled-gas stove and stainless steel sink. From the kitchen a new door led into a rough little lean-to room, built on at the rear of the building. So well ventilated that it was like stepping outside when you went into it, this was the lavatory. It contained a large can, like an oil barrel, with a lavatory seat on top, and a couple of sealed bottles of chemical fluid. Bess giggled when she saw the expression of distaste on Finn's face.

'It's better than Grandpa had,' she said teasingly.

To the front of the school, looking out onto the shore, were two bedrooms, each containing four small beds. It was clear that the recent visitors had not used the school at all, and, although dusty, everything was in good order. Finn liked the collections of silvery sea shells that lay on the window sills, and the jar of fragile, fawn dried grasses which a summer visitor had left on the kitchen table.

'I must say, I'm relieved,' confessed Bess, after she had looked around. 'I kept thinking about what Dan told us last night, and I was afraid we might find the place wrecked.'

'Oh, Dan's a terrible exaggerator,' said Douglas dismissively. 'The visitors probably lived on their yacht, and had a few picnics ashore.'

'Well, maybe,' replied Bess, not sounding convinced. 'It sounded more than that to me. But so far, so good. Now we'd better get this place cleaned up.'

'Cleaned up?' repeated Chris in astonishment. 'What on earth for? It looks perfectly clean to me.'

'To you, it would,' said Bess sweetly. 'To me, it doesn't. So here's a broom.'

Two minutes later, the boys were sweeping the bedrooms and making up beds, while Bess scrubbed the kitchen table, and Douglas got a peat fire going on the hearth which long ago had warmed the Hirsay children. When their tasks were finished, and Bess was preparing a late breakfast, Chris went out to look at the church. Finn sat on his bed, gazing out through the salt-blurred window at the sea. Down beyond the causeway, he could see spindrift over the breakers thudding on the rocks. He would have liked sunshine, but the bruised sky and inky sea did not disturb him. Like Bess, he had been relieved to find the school unvandalised, and hoped, with Douglas, that Dan had been exaggerating. But now he wanted to think of other things.

After breakfast, Douglas tactfully suggested that Finn might like to spend the rest of the morning looking at the remains of the village on his own, while the Coopers took a walk along the shore to the Pool of Seals. But

Finn would not have this.

'I want Chris to come with me,' he said. 'I want to show him things. OK, Chris?'

'Fine by me,' Chris agreed.

'Right,' said Douglas. 'Bess and I will walk to the Pool. We'll meet back here at twelve for a bite to eat, then we'll be off up the Red Hill to get the pathan.'

So Finn and Chris put on their jackets, and pushed themselves against the wind across Mr Ackerley's garden. First, they went to the little oval graveyard, stone-walled to keep out sheep evacuated with their owners sixty years before. Small, lichen-frosted tombstones tilted among the grass, but wind and rain had long ago rubbed out the names they bore. Yet Finn, who had imagined himself standing here, was glad that he had come.

'Let's go to Grandpa's cottage now,' he said to Chris, and with his friend plodding patiently beside him, he walked down through the old barley field, still spiked randomly by fragile, weedy stalks, descendants of seed the Islanders had planted. Ahead of them was the desolate huddle of ruined dwellings, unthatched and stripped to the bone by the weather. To Finn, this was the most important moment of his visit, and he thought how happy Grandpa would be to know that he was here.

'Do you know which one it is?' Chris asked.

Finn nodded. 'The last one in the row nearest the jetty, end-on to the sea,' he said.

They found it without difficulty. The village was very small. Finn stood for a moment outside, remembering it as he knew it had once been. He visualised the fire of peat burning on the hearthstone in the middle of the floor, the low chairs and the dresser made of driftwood by his great-great-grandfather, the precious flower-patterned china brought by his great-grandmother from Islay, when she came to Hirsay as a bride. That china was now in the kitchen at Corumbeg, as was the dark-cased pendulum clock which had ticked away the lives of those who had lived within these tumbled walls. Then Finn stepped reverently over the doorless threshold. He stopped so suddenly that Chris crashed into his back. They both stood silent for a moment, then Finn heard Chris swear and his own voice pleading, 'Oh, no. Please, not this.' Horror swept over him like sickness.

The mess in the cottage was appalling. People had been having a party, and the whole interior was awash with the filth and rubbish they had left behind. Beer cans, broken whisky bottles, eggshells and rusting tins were strewn everywhere. Food scraps had doubtless been eaten by birds, but charred chicken carcases lay on top of the dead embers of a fire. Soiled plastic bags had been blown to the back of the room, and caught between the rough stones. There they hung raggedly, like dismal flags.

Finn stood trembling, without will. It was Chris who acted.

'We'll clear it up,' he told Finn. 'Mum brought a roll of plastic sacks for rubbish. I saw them in a box when she unpacked.'

Now Chris was the leader, and Finn was too stunned to do anything but follow him. Walloped by the wind, they ran back to the school, where Chris found the roll of sacks, and detached four. He gave two to Finn, and they hurried back to the cottage. In silence, the two boys spent the next half-hour picking up every piece of rubbish, until Grandpa's cottage was clean and decent again. Finn was grateful to Chris, and thanked him warmly, but nothing could take away the painful feeling that the person he loved best had been cruelly dishonoured.

As the boys dragged the sacks back to the school, they met Douglas coming to look for them. He saw their faces, and understood without questioning. Taking two of the sacks, he said, 'I'm afraid they've been out along the rocks, too. Spray-paint, letters three feet high. Football slogans, and worse.'

Finn felt that he couldn't stand much more.

'Can we get it off?' he asked, near to tears.

Douglas put a sympathetic arm round his shoulders.

'I'm afraid not,' he said. 'We'll have to let the sea do the job for us, in its own time.' He shook his head, as if he were trying to rid himself of something horrible that had touched him. 'Even here,' he added helplessly. 'If only one could understand why.'

16 The Red Hill

When he set out after lunch, to climb the Red Hill with the Coopers, Finn believed that the most terrible thing that could possibly happen, had happened. In fact, there was worse to come.

Douglas carried, on a strap over his shoulder, a special box which Bess had brought for the pathan. It was made of wood, lined with plastic, and had two compartments. One was filled with damp compost for the plants, and had a glass top, to let in light. The other contained plastic jars for the seed-pods, which everyone was to help to gather.

They were, unexpectedly, a despondent group, their holiday already spoiled. Finn was devastated by what had happened in the morning, and the Coopers were sad for him, as well as depressed by the other vandalism they had discovered. They had agonised over it at lunch-time, unable to find any explanation which even began to make sense. It seemed that no key on earth could unlock the minds of people who could inflict such wounds on a beautiful place. The fact that they were probably drunk was the feeblest of excuses, and, as Bess said, calling them 'mindless' was ridiculous. Everybody has a mind. Only Chris, with bullies still in his thoughts, had a firm opinion.

'They just enjoy it,' he said. 'Bullies enjoy hurting

people. Vandals enjoy hurting the environment.' And when Douglas said that this was too simple an explanation, he added, 'You don't have a better one, Dad.' Regretfully, Douglas had to admit that this was true.

The vandals had climbed the Red Hill too, leaving a sporadic trail of chocolate wrappers and potato crisp bags, which had been impaled on the gorse bushes by the wind. Chris collected these, and put them in a sack. Finn knew that he should have helped him, but he couldn't be bothered, and even when Douglas pointed out to him a brown Hirsay mouse, twitching its whiskers under a bracken frond, he felt no thrill of delight. He could only think how nice it would be to go back to the school, get into bed, and pull the blankets right over his head. The weather matched his mood. The wind blew relentlessly from the sea, and the mauve sky promised rain.

Because it was flat, they came on the summit suddenly, like people stepping up onto a stage. And, because they hadn't been able to see it up ahead, they had no warning of what awaited them. That was why, just as Finn had been slow to take in what he was seeing earlier at Grandpa's cottage, they needed a moment now before their eyes transmitted to their brains the meaning of what they saw. Then came despair. The summit of the Red Hill had become a wasteland. Dan had not been exaggerating. This was the place of the fire he had seen from far out at sea.

It was obvious what had happened. Starting as a bonfire of heather and broom, the blaze had got out of control, and those who started it had no choice but to let it burn itself out. In every direction it had raged, devouring sea pink and chamomile, blaeberry and grass. Worst of all, its thousand tongues had licked eagerly into every crevice, right to the cliff edge, destroying the pathan which Bess had come so far to find. While Douglas and Chris stared numbly at the scorched rock and sooty, skeletal heather, Bess sat down with her back to the summit, and cried. Finn went and sat beside her. He had no words to comfort her, but when she couldn't find her handkerchief, he gave her his. Then it began to rain.

It was left to Douglas, who had experience of leading and encouraging others in bad circumstances, to get things under control.

'OK. There's no sense in hanging about here,' he said. 'Finn, Chris – you'd better have a squint down the cliffs while you have a chance. It's a sight worth seeing. Then we'll get back down.'

So Finn and Chris got down on their hands and knees, and crawled to the cliff edge, poking out their heads so that they could look down through the whirling snowstorm of wings, a thousand feet to the sea below. It was another of the things Finn had wanted to do, but the excitement was gone. He felt neither awed nor afraid.

Then they went down the hill, with the soft Atlantic rain blowing like wet cobwebs against their faces.

'The most infuriating thing,' Douglas remarked later, when they were eating corned beef and baked beans in the kitchen, by the light of a paraffin lamp, 'is that the plant is almost certainly growing in crevices on the cliffs – if only we could get down to it.' His dark eyes rested thoughtfully on a coiled rope which hung on a hook behind the door, but then he shook his head. 'Nothing to attach a rope to,' he said.

Bess was very tired, and disappointment excused the petulant look she gave him.

'Of course it must be growing on the cliffs,' she said irritably, 'but since there's no way on earth we could reach it, what's the point in talking about it? Do you think I'd allow anyone to risk his life for the sake of a few seeds? For God's sake, don't even think about it.'

Then, in the silence that followed, as the wind sobbed around the corners of the school, her vehemence subsided. Putting her head in her hands, she said, 'Oh, my dear, forgive me. This is all so terrible. First that cursed oil tanker off Newfoundland, and now this. I just can't believe that evil has triumphed again.'

At that moment, a kind of madness entered into Finn.

17   The Edge of the World

Very early in the morning, when Chris was still fast asleep, and the window was only a grey rectangle on the blackness of the wall, Finn slipped out of bed and dressed silently. On stockinged feet he tiptoed to the kitchen, took his boots from the line behind the door, and put them on. Then, slinging Bess's box over his shoulder, he carefully opened the door, and stepped out into the dawn.

Under the slaty sky, he moved quickly away from the school, flitted along the causeway like the memory of someone else, and struck up past the cottages towards the Red Hill. For the first time since yesterday morning, he felt peaceful, and full of resolve. He was going to do something good, to take away the stain which uncaring strangers had inflicted on his Island. He was going to do something heroic, for Grandpa, for Bess, and for the suffering people who needed pathan. At least, that was what he told himself, and only occasionally as he climbed, did that old, gratifying picture come to mind, Finn Lochlan alone in the newspaper photograph and an even more dramatic headline,

HIRSAY BOY RISKS LIFE FOR
WONDER PLANT

Not, he hastened to assure himself, that he was really risking his life at all. That was just the sort of exaggerated thing they liked to put in newspapers. When he had looked over the edge yesterday, Finn had seen that the cliff was not sheer, as it looked from the sea, but descended in a series of ledges. It had also seemed to him that there were plenty of hand and foot-holds in-between. Grandpa had often remarked that Finn had the strong hands and pliable, grasping toes which God had given to the Hirsay men so that they could climb rocks with ease, and now he would put them to the test. All he had to do was to keep a cool head, and find a ledge where he could safely sit and pick pathan out of the crevices in the rock. When he had filled his pockets, he would climb back up. It would be easy. He had not forgotten Bess's warning in the café at Oban. He just thought that he was less easily scared than she was. He was a boy of Hirsay, after all.

Finn went up quite quickly over the wet, springy turf, considering that he was hampered by the heavy box, and weary after a night when he had been kept awake by the fretful wind and sighing sea. The light intensified as he climbed, but the sun did not penetrate the cloud roof, and below him the Island lay enigmatically wrapped in mist. High up, the sound of the sea receded, to be replaced by the seabirds' cries which Finn would not admit were beginning to get on his nerves.

On the top, he did not give himself time to think. Stepping over the burnt grass to the cliff edge, he laid down Bess's box, then took off his boots and socks, because Islanders climbed barefoot. He went over backwards, feeling with his toes, then with his fingers for places to hold on. The wind sucked between his body and the cliff, which scared him a little, but he held on. He had descended perhaps five feet, and was just beginning to be pleased that he had got the hang of it, when the inevitable happened. The rock which his toes were probing moved, then cracked and fell away. Unable to bear the sudden weight of his swinging body, his fingers slipped too, and he fell.

Finn was more than lucky. A ledge, some ten feet further down, broke his fall, and he did not plunge a thousand feet to die, broken on cruel rocks. He was bruised and winded, but alive. Just being alive was enough for the first few minutes. Only after he had recovered his breath, and dared, very cautiously, to sit up, did he realise the terrible position he was in.

Looking up, he could see the cliff edge, not so very far off, but beyond his power to reach. A glance below made his head reel, and vomit rise in his throat. That was when he pressed back against the rock, closing his eyes against the menacing whirl of white wings, and experienced fear such as he had never known in his life before. No one, he thought, would ever find him. Douglas might come looking, and find the box, and his boots and socks, but he would think Finn had fallen to his death, and go away. The headline in the newspaper would say,

GLENAIRE BOY DIES
ON HIRSAY

That was what Granny and his father would see.

For the next hour and a half – although to him it seemed eternity – Finn huddled on the ledge, growing ever colder, his mind swinging between moments of hope, and long periods of despair. Surely Douglas would look over the edge, and perhaps spot him down below. Then he could run back to the school, and telephone the air and sea rescue station on the mainland. A helicopter would come ... That was a good thought, but a bad remembrance remorselessly wiped it out. This was the Island which was not marked on the map. It had never had a telephone, or a radio. There was no rescue that way.

Then Finn whimpered, and shook with fear, but after a while, optimism rose in him again. Douglas would not desert him. Perhaps he would come down to him on a rope. But, no. That would not do either. If the rock-face had not supported him safely, it would never bear a weight like Douglas's. Anyway, what was it Douglas had said last night at supper? 'Nothing to attach a rope to'. He would never take such a risk, and why should he? He had Bess and Chris to consider, and he was not Finn's father. For the first time in his life, Finn wanted his own father.

As time wore on, good thoughts died, and he was overwhelmed by hopelessness. He feared he would fall asleep, and roll over the edge. He would die of exposure, or be pecked to death by ferocious birds. Bitterly he cursed himself for his refusal to listen to the warning of people who knew that the natural world might be beautiful, but was not benign. Bess and Douglas had both tried to tell him. Hirsay is dangerous. It doesn't need people. Tears rolled down Finn's cheeks, and he put his arms over his head to protect himself from the slapping of wings. The drifting mist turned to rain.

'Finn! Finn! Can you hear me?' At first, through the hideous bird cry that ripped the air around him, Finn thought he was mistaken. But then it came again. 'Finn! Can you hear me?' It was Douglas. Then, 'Finn! Are you there?' That was Chris.

Joy knocked at Finn's heart, but he dared not let it in. He could hear them, but suppose that they couldn't hear him?

'Douglas!' he screamed. 'Douglas, I'm here, on a

ledge. Please, don't go away!'

He thought the wind had taken his words, and tossed them out to sea. But then he heard Douglas's deep voice again.

'OK, Finn. I hear you. Did you climb straight down from the box?'

'Yes!'

'Can you throw out your hanky or something, so that I can see where you are?'

Frantically, Finn fished in his pocket, and found a red handkerchief. Picking up a stone from the ledge, he wrapped the handkerchief round it and shouted. 'Now – I'll throw it now!'

The stone was a good idea. It went straight out for a bit, then the stone fell, and the handkerchief floated like a small red feather among the white. Finn heard Douglas again.

'OK. Hold on. We'll get you up.'

But how, Finn wondered, beginning to whimper again. Even if Douglas did climb down, and wanted to help him up, he would never have the courage to mount over these loose, treacherous rocks. If he slipped again ...

The silence stretched out, and Finn was sick with terror. They had gone away. He was alone again.

'Douglas!' he screamed.

'OK, Finn. I'm going to let down a rope. See if you can catch the end, then I'll tell you what to do next.'

Of course, Douglas would have brought a rope. Finn looked up, and saw it coming down. But the enemy wind snatched it, and it snaked away through the air, far out of his reach. It was pulled up again.

The next time the rope came down, it had Bess's box on the end to weight it, and Finn was able to grab the box, and draw it towards him. But by now his fingers were so numb with cold that he could hardly untie the knot around the strap, and when he did, the rope slipped from his fingers, floating wide again.

'Douglas, I dropped it,' he cried despairingly.

There was a pause. Then Douglas called, 'All right. Keep calm. Chris is coming down.'

Everything happened very quickly after that. Almost before he had time to be surprised, Finn saw two small, booted feet above him, then Chris was beside him on the ledge. His pale, pointed face was very intense. He had two ropes fastened around his waist, one of which he untied, and knotted expertly around Finn.

'Dad has both ropes tied round him,' he explained. 'He's going to pull us up one at a time, you first. You'll get bumped about a bit, but if you use your hands and feet to keep you off the rock, you'll be all right.' He looked at Finn's terrified face, and suddenly his serious expression was split by a grin. 'Oh, get on, Finn,' he said. 'You're perfectly safe. It's like being tied to the Statue of Liberty.'

So, because there was nothing else he could do, Finn got up on his knees, then onto his frozen feet.

'Ready?' asked Chris, and when Finn nodded, pulled lightly on his own rope.

Finn's rope went tight, and jerked under his armpits. A few painful seconds later he was up, and being dragged to safety over the cliff edge. As he rolled over, he saw Douglas's face above him, not delighted, or even relieved, but absolutely furious. Grabbing Finn by the shoulders, he tossed him violently down onto the wet black grass. Finn's rope came lashing down on top of him. Hurt and indignant, he watched Douglas brace himself again on the brink.

'OK, Chris,' he shouted. 'Ready? Up you come, boy.'

A moment later, Chris's damp brown head appeared over the edge. 'That was exciting,' he said cheerfully.

But Douglas had turned on Finn.

'You stupid little fool,' he said savagely. 'You made me risk my son.'

Then he wrapped Finn in a blanket, picked him up, and carried him down the hill.

18   Accident

Finn had only a vague memory afterwards, of being carried into the school, undressed by Bess in front of the fire, and rubbed down with warm towels. She gave him a hot drink, and escorted him to his bed. He could remember her shocked, unsmiling face, but little that she had said – or even if she had said much at all. He knew that he had tried to apologise to her for the loss of her box, because her reply, 'That's the least of my troubles,' stuck in his mind. Soon this would be all too true.

Finn fell asleep almost immediately, and did not wake until late in the afternoon. For the first time since their arrival, the sun had rubbed through the clouds, and a cone of watery light trembled between the window and his bed. He could hear voices outside, and as he turned over, he saw Bess and Chris pass the window in their waterproof jackets. Wide awake now, the recollection of his escapade pierced him, and he felt deeply ashamed.

He was wondering whether he should get up, go to find Douglas and say he was sorry, when Douglas appeared in the doorway. He was carrying a tray with a bowl of soup on it, and a piece of pie. He told Finn to sit up, and put the tray on his knees. 'Eat up,' he commanded. 'You must be ravenous.'

Finn realised that he was. He thought he would eat first and apologise later. He expected Douglas to go away, but Douglas sat down on Chris's bed, and watched him put the first spoonfuls of soup into his mouth.

'How do you feel now?' he asked.

'Glad I'm not dead,' said Finn.

'Yes, that's how we all feel,' Douglas agreed. He gave Finn a troubled look, and said, 'I'm sorry I shouted at you. Fear makes me angry.'

Finn felt his face going scarlet. The last thing he wanted was that Douglas should apologise to him.

'Don't,' he pleaded. 'I'm the one who's sorry. Dad says I'm a fool, and I am.'

A ghost of a smile passed over Douglas's lips, but he replied seriously, 'I've never thought so, although you were worse than foolish this time. We did try to warn you, but I suppose there are some things we have to find out for ourselves.

'I brought you here because I was worried that you lived in a dream world where Hirsay was concerned, and I didn't think it was good for you. I never meant you to have such a brutal awakening.'

'Is the pathan lost for ever?' Finn asked. 'I didn't see any growing when I was – down there. I didn't really look,' he added honestly.

This piece of absurdity almost made Douglas laugh, but he only answered the question.

'For ever's a long time,' he said. 'Nature heals its own wounds, when it can, and the kind of vandalism we've seen can only mark Hirsay in the short term. The sea will wash away the graffiti, and the grass on the hilltop will grow again. The plants on the cliffs will seed themselves, and one day pathan will grow where it can be reached. But not in time for Bess. Her boss has said that unless she can produce a reliable supply in three months, the project will be called off. We're not talking about months here, we're talking about years.'

'Poor Bess,' sighed Finn.

'Yes,' agreed Douglas. 'She hasn't had a good trip either. But at least we're all safe and sound. We'll have a nice supper, and in the morning, we'll go home. Nothing else can go wrong now.'

These, as it turned out, were fateful words. Hirsay had not done with them yet.

When Finn had finished eating, Douglas took the tray away, then made him take off his pyjama jacket. He ran his huge fingers over Finn's back and shoulders, pressing places and making Finn wince.

'You'll have some colourful bruises by tomorrow,' Douglas told him, 'but there's no worse harm done, thank God.' He then suggested that Finn might get up and dress, and come and help him lay the table for supper. 'Bess and Chris have gone for a walk along the shore while the tide's out,' he said. 'We'll eat when they get back. Could you manage the same again?'

'You bet,' Finn said.

He was grateful that Douglas hadn't reproached him, and was feeling much better as he laid out knives, forks and spoons. Douglas was stirring a pot of savoury soup on the stove, and supper seemed a pleasant prospect. Then suddenly there was an urgent sound of running footsteps outside. The door banged open, and Chris stood wide-eyed and panting on the threshold.

'Dad,' he gasped, 'come quickly! Mum slipped on the rocks, and she's hurt her ankle. She can't walk back. Please come.'

Douglas said nothing. In three strides he crossed the

kitchen, pushed Chris aside, and was out through the door. The boys heard his feet pounding away along the causeway, and looked at each other with apprehensive eyes.

'She thinks it's broken,' said Chris bleakly.

The next fifteen minutes were nightmarish. Finn took the soup off the heat, but couldn't think of anything else practical to do.

'Should we go and try to help?' he asked.

'No point,' Chris said. 'We'd just be in the way.'

They sat at the table, and as the minutes ticked icily by, Chris took dried grasses one by one from the jar, and picked them to shreds. Finn watched him.

At last they heard Douglas's steps again, and he came into the school, carrying Bess in his arms. He took her into their bedroom, and laid her on the bed. The boys followed, and hovered anxiously. Bess was white-faced, and absolutely furious.

'What an idiot I am,' she said through chattering teeth. 'How could I be so stupid?'

'You weren't stupid,' said Douglas tersely. 'Now pipe down, and let me get this boot off.'

He undid the lace, and gently drew the boot off Bess's foot. She could not hold back a yelp of pain. Chris ran into the kitchen, and Finn followed him.

'I'm not good at this sort of thing,' said Chris plaintively.

'Then keep out of the way,' growled Douglas, coming in behind him. The harshness in his voice startled Finn, until he remembered his words earlier, 'Fear makes me angry'. But then Douglas looked down into Chris's frightened face, and said more kindly, 'Listen. I need you to help me. Bring me a bundle of cotton sleeping bags from the cupboard in your bedroom, and fetch a bowl of cold water. Finn, you make Bess a mug of tea. Then I want you to have your supper, and keep yourselves amused. Mum and I don't want to be interrupted for a bit. OK?'

Having a job to do steadied Chris. He went off to look for the sleeping bags, and Douglas departed to Mr Ackerley's outhouse, to fetch a piece of wood for a splint. While he was waiting for the kettle to boil, Finn went in and spoke to Bess.

'Does it hurt badly?' he asked, looking at her bare, twisted right foot.

'Not yet,' she said wryly. 'I'm an even bigger fool than you are, Finn.'

'Thanks,' said Finn, 'but that would be impossible.'

Fortunately, Douglas was trained in first aid, and knew what to do. While the boys made a pretence of eating supper and playing chess, he applied cold compresses to Bess's ankle, and splinted her leg with a strip of wood, and bandages which he made by tearing up the sleeping bags. When the boys were allowed in to see her, she was lying on the bed in her nightdress, with her foot on a pillow. She managed to smile at them, and say firmly to Chris, 'I'm all right now. It doesn't hurt much, and as soon as we get to Oban, Dad will take me to hospital to get a plaster put on. It's an awful nuisance, but it isn't a disaster. It's just a good thing that Dan's coming to fetch us in the morning.'

Chris went to bed comforted. But Bess was wrong. The storm which Dan had said was unlikely before mid-November was already on its way. He would not come to fetch them in the morning.

19   'People are like Butterflies'

Around midnight, the wind changed its tune. Its usual monotonous singing rose with a loud, strumming accompaniment to a banshee cry, which seemed to call up all the other winds of the ocean. Howling triumphantly, they threw themselves upon the Island, rousing the sea to fury, and hurling rain like handfuls of pebbles against the windows of the school. Doors and window-frames rattled wildly, and the boys, quaking in bed, felt the whole building shudder as the storm thudded against it.

Under the door, they could see a glimmer of light from the lamp which Douglas kept lit in the other bedroom. Closer to hand than the storm, they could hear him moving around, and knew that neither he nor Bess could sleep. Occasionally, he came into their room, and said comforting things like, 'It's all right. You're perfectly safe,' and, 'It's only a storm. It'll die down by morning.'

But when Chris quavered, 'I want Mum,' he replied firmly, 'Sorry, old man. She doesn't want you.'

Like so many predictions during the last few days, this latest one of Douglas's was mistaken. Dawn came, lightening fractionally the window shape on the wall, but the storm raged on. Hope died. They would not get off the Island that day.

Or the next. For forty-eight terrible hours, they were holed up in the school, unable even to open the door because of the ferocity of the gale, and the waves which thundered over the causeway to wash the walls of the school. They were prisoners, of forces that could not know what pity was.

Douglas moved Bess's bed into the kitchen, so that she could be near the fire. Alternately she sweated and shivered, and although on the first day she tried to be cheerful, and chat to Douglas and the boys, by the second she hadn't the strength. She lay with her eyes closed, and when they spoke to her, she answered vaguely, as if they were strangers. Her ankle swelled monstrously, and when Douglas had given her all the aspirins in the first aid kit, there was little more he could do to ease her pain. Chris's face had a pinched, frightened look, and Finn, himself sore, stiff, and stupid through lack of sleep, had a hard time trying to cheer him up.

By the second day, there was another problem. Supplies of food, peat and paraffin were beginning to run low. Douglas, who had encouraged and cared for them all heroically, looked strained, and for the first time close to despair.

'If this goes on until tomorrow,' he said, 'I'll have to break into the Ackerleys' place, and see if they left any tins behind.'

These words roused Bess for the first time in many hours. She opened terrified eyes, and said violently, 'You'll do no such thing. You're not going out in a storm like that, Douglas. Even you would be swept away.'

'All right, my love,' said Douglas soothingly. 'Maybe it won't be necessary.'

Finn went into his bedroom, and lay down on his bed. Outside, the wind howled, and the salt sea spray ran down the window like tears. And there, in the dark little room, a tiny seed of suspicion, sown in his mind at Corumbeg on the night when he had wondered how Grandpa really felt about being illiterate, grew into a hideous flower of certainty. Grandpa had not told him the truth about that, or about anything else concerning Hirsay. The truth was what he was experiencing now, and Grandpa's stories were just a barrel of moonshine.

Hirsay was not a golden summer isle, where Islanders lived happy, fulfilled lives. It was an isolated, inhospitable rock, where for centuries people had risked their lives to feed their children, where their crops could be destroyed in a single night, where supplies from the mainland depended upon the whim of the sea. They had looked starvation in the face, as Finn and the Coopers were doing now.

He thought what it must really have been like, in such a storm as this, sheltering in a poor cottage like the one he had visited yesterday. Grandpa had made it sound such fun, the boy playing with Gruach before the fire, while the father wove tweed at the loom, and the mother sat in her low chair with her knitting. Now Finn could only imagine the smoke, the stink of fish and fulmar oil, the family huddling terrified as the wind screamed, and tried to tear away the thatch above their heads.

He saw the Islanders dirty, disadvantaged and ignorant, living all their lives in fear of the experiences he and Bess had endured here, a fall from the cliff, a serious accident when you couldn't even get a message to the nearest doctor on Lewis, sixty miles away. Finn remembered Douglas's words, 'People are like butterflies on Hirsay', and for the first time he understood what they meant. But why had Grandpa misled him? That was a pain and a mystery beyond understanding.

But now the ordeal was nearly over. That evening the wind began to die down. In the early hours of the morning, the sea receded, and the storm blew itself away into the Atlantic. Finn and Chris slept, and when Douglas woke them at seven o'clock, they saw Hirsay washed, and shining serenely in the morning sun.

'We must have breakfast and get packed up,' Douglas told the boys. 'Dan will be here for us as soon as he can.'

Two hours later, sitting on the pile of rucksacks on the jetty, Finn and Chris saw the *Harebell*, far out to sea.

20   Granny's Box

After two years of longing to leave, Finn could scarcely believe how glad he was to be back at Corumbeg. It was dark when they arrived, but from far down the valley he could see the light in the kitchen window, piercing the night like a single star. When he ran indoors, and saw the old, familiar furniture, and smelt the familiar smells, he knew that this was really home.

It had been a long, long day. Dan had helped Douglas carry Bess on board the *Harebell*, and as Hirsay gathered itself back into mystery on the horizon, made an SOS call on his radio. At Oban, an ambulance had been waiting to take Bess to the West Highlands Hospital, where, in the early evening, Douglas and the boys were allowed to spend ten minutes at her bedside. Although sleepy from the anaesthetic, she knew what she wanted, and insisted that Douglas should take Finn and Chris to Corumbeg immediately.

'I'll be perfectly all right, once I get a decent sleep,' she said, 'but poor Colin and Frances must be desperate to see Finn safe and sound. You must get him back to them, Douglas, as soon as you possibly can.'

Douglas, who had slept on the *Harebell*, reluctantly agreed with this, so after they had said goodbye to Bess, he bundled the boys into the car, and drove through the night to Glenaire. Mr Lochlan and Granny had heard reports of the great storm on the radio, and realising that the Hirsay party was stranded in the school, had not expected to have Finn back on Monday. They had been very relieved, however, to have a telephone call from Douglas earlier in the day, and they were delighted to see Finn now. Since it was after midnight, the boys were fed and sent straight to bed, but Granny, Mr Lochlan and Douglas sat up until two o'clock, and next morning there was little about the Island visit which had not been discussed, except for Finn's ordeal on the cliff. It was typical of Douglas that he felt Finn should handle that in his own way.

Actually, Finn had hoped to get away with saying nothing about it at all. He could see no point. But unfortunately Granny had an annoying habit of never knocking on doors, and next morning she walked in on Finn before he had put on his shirt.

'Good heavens, child,' she said in horror, staring at the bruises on his back and shoulders. 'What on earth have you done?'

Very unwillingly, Finn told her. He knew she'd have it out of him, sooner or later. Her trembling hands, and expression of grief for what might have been, hurt him more than if she had boxed his ears.

What he would remember all his life, however, was the look on his father's face when he was forced by Granny to repeat his story at breakfast-time. Finn had often thought that his father did not care for him, but now the intense anguish in Mr Lochlan's dark eyes, the movement of his prominent Adam's apple as he swallowed dryly, convinced him that he was mistaken. Through all his guilt and embarrassment, Finn felt a surge of happiness. Douglas Cooper was not the only man who feared to risk his son.

At ten o'clock, a triumphant Bess telephoned to tell Douglas that she had persuaded the doctor at the hospital to let her go home. He had agreed to send her to Glasgow in an ambulance that afternoon.

'We'd best be off, then,' said Douglas, coming back into the kitchen. 'I'll have to get the house opened up, and do a bit of shopping. Bring your rucksack down, Chris, and put Shep in the car.'

For all his pleasure in being home, Finn watched desolately as the blue car rocked slowly down the hill. He stood at the gate until it disappeared among the conifers on the Glen Road, then turned and went back indoors. He felt empty, as if all that had sustained him had been washed away, and he had nothing with which to replace it.

Granny understood how it was with him. Although all she said was, 'You'll feel better when you're back at school,' she baked butterscotch cookies for him in the afternoon, and made his favourite macaroni cheese for supper. Afterwards, he said he was tired, and would have an early night, but upstairs in his room, the sight of Chris's empty camp-bed made him feel lonelier than ever. The Hirsay map, now so poignant and so meaningless, intensified his sense of emptiness. Tomorrow, he would take it down.

When Granny arrived with the cocoa, Finn saw on the tray, beside the mugs, a shabby red tin box. It seemed vaguely familiar to him, but in his present mood, he couldn't even be bothered to ask what was in it. Granny handed him his mug, and sat down on the end of his bed. She looked at him for a moment in her cock-headed, bird-eyed way, then she asked carefully, 'Do I gather that Hirsay wasn't a great success? Falling down cliffs and broken ankles apart, I mean.'

Finn avoided her eye.

'No. It wasn't really,' he said.

Granny nodded thoughtfully.

'I used to think,' she said, 'when I was young, that I'd like to go once – just to see it, because it meant so much to your Grandpa. But he never wanted to go back, and later on, I realised why. It had become a different Island in his mind, you see, and he was afraid of the reality. He couldn't face the possibility that he would see it as you've seen it. So it was better for him not to go.'

Finn was silent, then suddenly it all came tumbling out.

'Oh, Granny, it was such a terrible place. It must have been so awful living there. It's so lonely, and dangerous, and the storm – it was absolutely terrifying. We hardly ever saw the sun, until the morning we left. Then it was beautiful, but when I thought of all the dreadful things that had happened there, I hated it. And I can't understand why Grandpa lied to me.'

As he spoke these dreadful words, he saw Granny wince, and screw up her eyes, as if he had struck her in the face. 'Oh, no, I didn't mean that,' he added hastily. 'Sorry, Granny.'

But Granny looked at him gravely, and said, 'Don't apologise, Finn. If that's how you feel, I'd rather know, then I can try to explain.' She paused, sighed, and then continued, 'Try to look at it like this. All old people believe that in their childhood everything was better than it is now. They think that summers were warmer, and the snow more beautiful. They think that potatoes tasted better, and plums were twice the size. I'm like that myself. Grandpa told it to you the way he remembered it, with the sun shining on the Red Hill, and the seals swimming off Hamasgeir. The storms he remembered sixty years back had lost their terror, and the food he ate when he was ten tasted delicious in his memory, although he'd have been absolutely revolted if I'd ever served it up for his supper.'

Finn considered this. 'Yes, I do see,' he said.

'Do you?' Granny asked. 'I hope you do. I often thought that Grandpa was wrong to involve you in his memories as much as he did. At your age, you should be eager for the future, not living in a past to which no one could seriously want to return. Perhaps it was an unwise game. But to say that he lied to you is cruel, and far too strong a way of putting it.'

Finn saw how badly he had hurt her, and he would have done anything to take his words back. He could only say remorsefully, 'I'm very sorry I said that. I really didn't mean it. But I've been so mixed-up, Granny. I'd never thought before how hard it must have been, living in these poor wee houses, and not having a doctor, or any proper education. Although I did think about education, when I saw how much Chris cared about not being able to read.'

Granny nodded. 'Yes. It was a harsh, difficult life in many ways,' she agreed. 'The loss of education was the worst of it, I think, not only because it put Grandpa at such a disadvantage when he came off the island. If people can read, they can experience the world through books, even on an island like Hirsay. It's too easy to say Grandpa wouldn't have known what he was missing. That's a poor argument. He'd have been missing it all the same.'

It went through Finn's head that she really was a sensible old bird. But he remained silent, and she went on, 'Still, for all that I've never been a Hirsay fan, there were good things about life there too, Finn – things we've lost, and must get back, if our planet is to survive. For example, the Islanders shared all they had, and they cared for one another. They didn't pollute the Island, or take from it more than they needed. These were lessons Grandpa learned when he was a child, and that's why he was the good man he was.' Suddenly she smiled, and added, 'And often the sun did shine, and the seals basked, and children played games and paddled in the rock-pools. I admit that Grandpa painted too rosy a picture, but you're in danger of painting one too black. Try to believe in something in-between.'

'I'll do that,' promised Finn. But just as he was beginning to feel better, the memory of the burnt hilltop, and Grandpa's cottage strewn with rubbish, blew on him like a sad sigh.

'Oh, Granny,' he cried. 'There was no pathan, and the mess in his cottage — '

Douglas had warned her, and she had a reply ready.

'It was very tragic that the pathan was destroyed,' she said. 'I just wonder whether the people who did it would have thought twice if they'd known what they were doing. Vandals and litter-louts never think of the consequences, and that's one of the problems your generation will have to tackle. But as for the cottage – well, it doesn't matter to Grandpa now. And wasn't it wonderful that you were there to clear it up? Can you imagine how that would have pleased him?'

Suddenly, a great burden seemed to roll away from Finn. He wanted more than anything to say something to Granny that would please her, and make up for the horrible thing he had said.

'You know, Granny,' he said, 'Grandpa must have been very brave, I think. If you saw those cliffs he climbed to collect the eggs — '

He broke off as a most peculiar expression, a mixture of astonishment, incredulity and amusement, appeared on Granny's face. Amusement must have been the strongest, because she began to laugh. Finn watched her rocking to and fro on her thin bottom, clutching her ribs as tears of mirth ran down her face, and for a moment he seriously wondered if she had gone mad.

But eventually she pulled herself together and gasped, 'Oh, Finn! Did he tell you he did that? Then he really was a fibber after all. No one had climbed cliffs on Hirsay for years – one of the reasons they had to leave was that they'd become far too dependent on supplies coming from the mainland. But Grandpa! He never climbed a cliff in his life. He couldn't stand heights. He was dizzy if he looked out of the attic window.'

At first, Finn was dumbfounded. Then indignant. But finally he laughed too. And, as clearly as if he had just come into the room, he seemed to see Grandpa, with his white hair and kind face, and mischievously twinkling blue eyes. You old rascal, thought Finn. I bet you weren't descended from a Viking at all. I'd give you a piece of my mind if I had you here. But then he remembered that he hadn't thought any the less of Douglas, after he had learned that he could make an ass of himself. It would be like that with Grandpa too.

'What's in that box?' he asked, with a stirring of interest in ordinary things.

Granny turned to lift the red tin box from the tray on Finn's desk, and laid it on his lap.

'I found this in the bottom of my wardrobe, while you were away,' she told him. 'It belonged to Grandpa. It stood on the mantelpiece in his mother's kitchen until he married me, then it stood on our kitchen mantelpiece all though our life together. Do you remember it in the Glasgow house?'

'I think so,' replied Finn.

'I don't know when it was last opened,' continued Granny, 'but it holds the things that Grandpa gathered on top of the Red Hill, the day he left Hirsay, all those years ago. I thought you might like to have them now.'

'Oh yes, I would,' said Finn gratefully.

It was difficult to get the lid off the box, because it was jammed on so tightly, but at last he levered it up, and tipped out the contents onto his quilt. There was a white feather, a smooth black stone, a strand of grey sheep's wool, and a brown snail shell, with a cream whorl. There was also a small envelope, once white, now yellow with age.

'I wonder what this is?' said Finn, picking it up. 'Look, it's got writing on it.'

Granny leaned forward, and together they read, in the painstaking printing which was the nearest Grandpa got to writing, these words: 'Seeds of the pathan I gathered on Cnoc Ruadh, Hirsay, on 5th September, 1929. JL.'

Very carefully, with trembling fingers, Finn tore along the top of the envelope, and opened it out. In the bottom lay the fragile remains, like dried insects' wings, of some seed pods, and about half a teaspoonful of tiny black seeds.

21   Seed Time

'Granny, please, am I allowed to 'phone Bess now?'

Finn had been asking this question since half-past seven in the morning, while the minute hand of the Hirsay clock ticked slowly round the yellow moon face, with its usual indifference to human impatience. And always the answer was the same. 'No, Finn. I've told you. Not before ten.'

Mr Lochlan, consulted before he went out to work, had looked at the tiny seeds with an interest which surprised Finn. Then he had said, 'Yes, it's possible. They've been kept perfectly dry, so they probably could grow, in the right conditions. I remember reading somewhere that when they excavated one of the pyramids in Egypt, they found some seed corn which had been buried with the Pharaoh. When they planted it, it grew.'

'After how long?' Finn wanted to know.

'About four thousand years, I suppose,' replied his father. 'So after sixty, I should think these are in with a chance. You'd better 'phone Bess and tell her, and ask if she wants us to post the seeds to her.'

Which was what Finn wanted to do, more than anything else in the world at that moment, only Granny wouldn't let him.

'Bess will be very tired this morning, and her ankle

will be sore,' she explained. 'It really wouldn't be fair to disturb her before ten o'clock.'

So Finn, who was having Friday at home to recover from his adventure, had to hang about in the kitchen, doing a crossword and reading old comics, until, at five to ten, Granny took pity on him.

'All right,' she said, amused by his desperation. 'If it'll put you out of your misery, I think you could 'phone now.' Finn was out of the room, across the hall and dialling the Coopers' number, almost before she had finished speaking.

Chris answered, sounding very perky. Perhaps relief had something to do with it, or perhaps he was just pleased because he was having an extra day off school as well.

'Good morning. Three-three-one, four-nine-two-seven,' he said importantly. 'Who's calling, please?'

'It's me,' said Finn impatiently, 'so you can cut out the posh stuff. I want to speak to Bess.'

'Oh, do you?' sniffed Chris, trying to sound haughty. But he couldn't keep it up. He giggled, and said, 'Well, you're just in time. She has to start hopping to the Infirmary in twenty minutes, to have a check-up. What do you want to speak to her about?' he asked inquisitively.

'Mind your own business,' said Finn smartly. He had no intention of telling his magic news to anyone but Bess. 'Just put her on, will you?'

Chris made a rude noise into the receiver. 'OK,' he said. 'You're a mean pig, but I'll tell her. She's got a 'phone in the bedroom. But be warned – she's very peevish.'

There was an irritatingly long delay, during which Finn could hear the Coopers' radio, and a lorry thundering past their house in University Avenue. Then there was a click, and Bess's voice came on the line, not sounding peevish at all. 'Hi, Finn. How are you?'

Finn thought afterwards that it would have been polite to ask how she was, and say he hoped her ankle was a little better today, but at the time he didn't even think of it. He heard his own voice, shrill with excitement. 'Bess! I've got some seed ...' Then he began to pour out his story.

Bess listened in complete silence, and at the end he had to say, 'Are you still there?'

'Yes,' she said faintly. 'I'm still here.' In a voice struggling to keep calm, she went on, 'Finn, listen carefully. This is what you've got to do. Get Dad to take you to a garden shop. Buy a bag of seed compost, and a seed propagator with a clear plastic lid. Then — '

'Hold on a minute,' Finn interrupted. 'Dad said I was to ask you if you wanted us to send you the seeds by post.'

He heard Bess breathe in, but if she was tempted, she put the temptation aside.

'No,' she said. 'It's kind of you to offer, but they're your seeds, Finn. Yours and your Grandpa's. You must get them to grow.' And she gave him the rest of the instructions.

When Mr Lochlan came in to lunch, he was almost as excited as Finn.

'There's a garden centre at Kinross, just along the road,' he said, with satisfaction. 'We'll go this afternoon.'

So they did, and bought the compost, and a propagator. Then they went to the Little Chef restaurant, and had tea, and bacon and eggs, and bread and butter, and a slice of apple pie each. They talked about the farm, and what they were going to do there, and how the future would be different from the past. And they apologised to each other for the last time.

When they got home, they planted the seeds together, and put them in a warm place near the kitchen window. Then they began to wait.

22   Harvest

October drifted into November. A dust of snow blew across the hilltops, and a night of high wind brought down the leaves. Finn went to Glasgow to spend a weekend with the Coopers, and it was arranged that they would all come to Corumbeg for Christmas. Chris said this would be a pleasant change from a tent on Rannoch Moor. Bess's ankle slowly mended, and Finn went on watering the seeds.

As the terrible events on Hirsay receded, Grandpa began to take his place in Finn's memory as someone who would always be loved, but who now belonged to the past. His goodness was cherished, his fault of exaggeration forgiven, and Finn was at last able to live in the present, and look forward to the future. He did not take down the Hirsay map and pictures, which now became a natural part of his life, a reminder of Grandpa, and the happy times they had spent together. Nowadays, however, the pictures of the pirates and the Blue Men merely made him laugh. He had had real adventures on Hirsay which made all imaginary adventures tame by comparison. But he was not aware that his hatred of the Island was fading, until one day he surprised himself by thinking that he might like to visit it again.

But the seeds did not grow.

'It's far too early to start getting despondent,' Bess

assured him, in the last week of November. 'They had the devil of a job in Canada getting the seeds to germinate at all. Keep them warm. Make sure they're getting enough light, and not too much water, and we'll see.'

She did not tell Finn that she had heard from one of her colleagues at the lab, that the Canadian scientists had abandoned their attempt to grow pathan. The action was all in the kitchen at Corumbeg now.

In spite of Bess's encouragement, however, Finn was finding it hard not to be pessimistic. But then something wonderful happened.

The second of December was Chris's twelfth birthday. He had made sure that everyone at Corumbeg was aware of this occasion, so that, he said cheerfully, they could all send him cards. The difference between the present merry, friendly Chris and the sorrowful creature they had first known was so satisfying that this piece of cheek was forgiven him. Granny knitted him a blue and white woolly hat for ski-ing, and Finn made him a card with a picture of two legs and skis sticking out of a snowdrift. Even Mr Lochlan bought a card at Yett Post Office. These were sent off in good time. The birthday treat, which included Finn, was to be a visit to the pantomime in the Christmas holidays.

In the evening, Chris rang up to say, 'Thank you,' but as he stuttered out his thanks, Finn sensed that he was as excited as Finn had been on the day when he had told Bess about the seeds.

'What's up, Chris?' he asked suspiciously.

'Oh, Finn,' squeaked Chris. 'You'll never guess what I got for my birthday!'

'What?'

'Frandy!'

'Frandy,' repeated Finn, mystified. 'What on earth's Frandy?' He wondered if it was a game, or a new kind of chocolate bar he hadn't heard of.

'Frandy Farm,' yelled Chris. 'You must know, Finn. You pass the road-end every morning going to school. It's that grey house between Middle Corum and Yett reservoir. Mum and Dad have bought it, and I got a picture of it in my birthday card. We'll be coming to live there in the spring. I'll be able to go to school with you, and Dad will be able to work with Colin, and I'll be able to have reading lessons with Granny again. Oh, Finn, isn't it great?'

Finn was so pleased that he could hardly find words to say so. Then Douglas came on the line, and said he wanted to talk to Colin.

Next day, as if they were warmed by the glow of happiness at Corumbeg, the seeds began to grow. First, Finn saw two tiny wisps of lime, then half a dozen, and within a week a thin green fur spread over the compost in the propagator. Bess cried when she heard, and so did Granny.

'If only Grandpa could have known,' she said.

On the night when the first proper leaves became visible, Mr Lochlan came up to Finn's room when he was in bed. Finn could not remember his ever coming before, and he was surprised, but pleased too. Mr Lochlan sat down on the stool, stretching out his long legs in front of him. He looked pensively at the Hirsay map, and the beautiful pictures around it. Finn lay watching his father's face, waiting to find out why he had come.

Eventually Mr Lochlan said slowly. 'It's a bad thing – to live in the past too much. Do you think you've got

126

over it?'

Finn, who had got over it some time ago, felt a sharp, sudden affection for his father. Trust him, he thought, to start worrying, long after there had ceased to be anything to worry about.

'Oh, yes,' he said. 'Have you?'

He saw his father twitch, and the slight bristling of the dark moustache which was comical, but slightly scary too. In the past, it had usually been the prelude to some snubbing or other. But now Mr Lochlan said quite mildly, 'How do you mean?'

Finn had started, so he might as well go on. 'Oh, you know,' he said. 'Virgil, and that farm in Italy. That was your Hirsay, wasn't it?'

There was a pause, then his father grinned at him. But, 'Point taken,' was all he said.

He sat on for a while, still looking at the map, and then said tentatively, 'I was wondering. There's an advertisement in *Farming Today* for volunteers to go to Hirsay next summer, to help rebuild the church. Some chap, Ackerley, who owns the place, wants to restore the whole settlement eventually, as a base for people interested in conservation, and studying the environment. I thought – if you liked – you and I might go for a fortnight, and give a hand. We're almost Islanders, after all.'

Then Finn knew that he really did want to give Hirsay a second chance. It was still Grandpa's Island, and it would be fun to go with his father, now that it was no longer the hub of his world. Perhaps this time the sun would shine.

'Just the two of us?' he asked.

'That's what I'd like.'

'So would I,' said Finn. But then the thought of all

the work they would have to do at Corumbeg next year made him add, 'But remember, only for a fortnight, Dad. We'll be far too busy to be away for longer than that.'

The noise Mr Lochlan made began as a snort, but ended as a proper laugh. He got up to go, but as he opened the door, he turned and said, 'One other thing. If you can spare the time from your farming on Saturday, would you like to drive down to Kelso with me, to look at some collie pups? It's time we were training a dog, if we're going to take over the sheep from Tam in the spring.'

'Good idea,' said Finn happily. 'And we'll call it Gruach. That was the name of Grandpa's dog, on Hirsay, long ago.'